THE NEIGHBOR IS NIXED

A HUMOROUS PARANORMAL COZY MYSTERY

CARLY WINTER

Edited by
DIVAS AT WORK EDITING
Cover by
COVEREDBYMELINDA.COM

WESTWARD PUBLISHING / CARLY FALL, LLC

Copyright © 2021 by Carly Winter

All rights reserved.

No part of this book may be reproduced in any form or by any electronic or mechanical means, including information storage and retrieval systems, without written permission from the author, except for the use of brief quotations in a book review.

This is a work of fiction. Unless otherwise indicated, all the names, characters, businesses, places, events and incidents in this book are either the product of the author's imagination or used in a fictitious manner. Any resemblance to actual persons, living or dead, or actual events is purely coincidental.

Cover by: CoveredbyMelinda.com

THE NEIGHBOR IS NIXED

Love thy neighbor... or kill them?

When the house across the street sells and Sylvia moves in, Bernie's quiet neighborhood is turned upside down.

Demanding, rude and determined to have things her way, Sylvia threatens to have Bernie's bed and breakfast shut down while also making life difficult for the other neighbors.

Just as the residents come together to fight the offending newcomer, she's found murdered. The suspect list is long, but since Bernie has the most to lose, the Sheriff has her in his sights.

Can Bernie and her ghostly grandmother, Ruby, solve the killing before she's arrested for a crime she didn't commit?

CHAPTER 1

As I drove my SUV down the street toward my home, I kept my eye on my new neighbor's house and whispered a curse when I noted her car in the driveway. Sylvia had moved in a couple of months ago and for various reasons, I'd been avoiding her ever since. Mainly, she simply wasn't a nice person. Secondly, she'd threatened to have my bed and breakfast shut down. When I didn't see her in her front yard, I accelerated the car and rounded my home into the back lot. I almost expected her to be waiting for me there as she had once this past month, but thankfully, all I discovered was dirt and the desert that stretched behind my house.

With a sigh, I parked and entered my home,

my arms loaded with groceries. My ghostly grandmother, Ruby, waited for me in the kitchen with her hands clasped in front of her and wearing a scowl along with her purple muumuu.

"You're late," she grumbled. "You said you'd only be gone an hour."

"I know. I think they're short-staffed at the store. Checkout took forever."

"Okay, I forgive you then. When can we go riding?"

I smiled to bite back my irritation. For Christmas, I'd bought a new ATV to replace Ruby's, which I'd had to sell to make ends meet when I first moved to Sedona and didn't know she still resided on this plane. The new one was red with the name *Bolt* painted across the side. Her old one had been named *Flash*, but *Bolt* conveyed speed, and also the lightning bolt that had struck me, scrambling my brains so I could finally see Ruby.

Like I had nothing better to do than to take my grandmother out on our ATV. Forget bills, keeping the lights on, and annoying things like eating. Ruby just wanted to ride and pestered me frequently, to the point where I was regretting my purchase.

"Maybe later today," I said. "I have guests

coming tomorrow and need to make sure the rooms are in order."

"You did that after the last ones left."

"That was two weeks ago," I replied, shoving the bottle of wine and gallon of almond milk into the refrigerator. "You know I like to double-check everything before new arrivals."

The break from guests had been nice, but I also looked forward to the boost in my bank account after the next batch came. All three rooms would be filled with visitors for a local wedding, a total of six adults and one toddler staying with me. Speaking of which… where had I placed the blow-up bed? I'd promised it to the kids' parents so all three didn't have to sleep together.

"Okay, fine," Ruby said with a long sigh. "I'll sit here and watch you while I die a slow death of boredom."

"I hate to remind you, but you're already dead," I replied. "Too bad you're such a lame ghost. If you could move inanimate objects, you could help me."

"I'd rather be lame than wield a vacuum."

"And I'd rather not listen to you complain about how boring your life is," I said. "I'm doing the best I can to make a living. Sorry, but keeping you entertained is not a high priority for me right now."

Ruby grumbled something about spending too much money while alive, then disappeared, leaving me to my tasks.

I finished putting away the groceries and set off to get the house cleaned. After oiling the banister, mopping the kitchen floor, and studying each guest room with a critical eye, I checked the supplies of toilet paper and towels in each room. My last guests had decided they appreciated my towels so much, they'd stolen three of them. So now, instead of leaving extras, I only stacked the amount equal to the number of people staying in the room. If they wanted extras, they'd have to ask. As with everything in life, it was always one jerk who ruined everything for everyone.

Just as I shut the door to the last bedroom, Ruby yelled *Boo!* from behind me, causing me to yelp and drop my carrier of cleaning supplies. She snorted and giggled as if it was the funniest thing she'd ever seen.

"I've asked you not to do that," I said, bending over and picking up my canisters and cloths. "Many times."

"And I've asked you to take me on an ATV

ride," Ruby replied, crossing her arms over her chest. "Many times."

"Ruby, I—"

"Never mind. I know you're busy. I'm not here to fight. Although, I do have to admit I love scaring you."

Standing, I picked up my carrier and glared at my ghost. "If you aren't here to argue, what do you want?"

"I forgot to tell you LaLa came by. I think she left something in the door."

LaLa, otherwise known as Yolanda to everyone but Ruby, was one of my neighbors. We'd only recently become friendly.

Huh. Wonder what she wanted? "I'll go down and check."

Hopefully it wasn't an invitation to a block party or something similarly horrid. I liked my neighbors, but I also liked staying home more. The older I became, the more social situations seemed to stress me out.

After hustling down the stairs and putting away my cleaning supplies, I opened the front door. A note had been shoved in between the door and jamb.

. . .

Hi Bernie –

We're having a neighborhood meeting about Sylvia. I'm not sure what we we're going to do, but she's now threatened bodily harm to Wilder with a shovel. We're discussing getting the cops involved and maybe hiring a lawyer. This afternoon at four, my house.

Yolanda

I SHOOK MY HEAD. Staying out of that one.

"What does it say?" Ruby asked.

After I read it out loud, her eyes widened. "We're going, right?"

"No."

"Why not?"

"I don't want to get involved," I said. "It's one thing for Sylvia to complain about a tree, but quite another for her to threaten someone with a shovel. I'm sure Wilder can take care of himself. I don't want her coming at me with a makeshift weapon."

"You have to go," Ruby said. "It'll be the most exciting thing that's happened around here since Christmas."

"No. I'm doing fine dealing with Sylvia in my own way."

"You mean by avoiding her?"

"Exactly."

Ruby rolled her eyes. "You can't go through the rest of your life looking out your window before you leave your house so you can dodge your neighbor."

The thought had occurred to me as well, and I'd be willing to give it a shot if it meant eluding confrontation. "Maybe she'll move soon." I held up Yolanda's note. "She's angered the rest of the neighborhood to the point they're discussing legal action. They'll chase her out."

"You hope. You can't know that for sure."

"Yes, I *hope* they do."

"I'm not sure what legal grounds they have to do that, but I'd love to go the meeting and find out," Ruby said, smiling sweetly and batting her eyelashes.

"Oh, give me a break," I said with a snort. "You couldn't care less about anything having to do with legal issues. You want to go for a front row seat to the drama that may ensue."

She shrugged. "That's always fun as well. But we watch a lot of cop shows. Maybe we could come up with some ideas for the crew ready to take on Slimy Sylvia."

"I'm keeping my nose out of it," I replied. "That's the end of the conversation."

As I turned and headed back into the kitchen, a knock sounded on the front door. Ruby glanced out the window and whooped with excitement. "It's Sheriff Bruce Walker looking sexier than Brad Pitt on a good day!"

Sexy would never be a word I could use to describe the seventy-year-old man with a full head of gray hair, but Ruby had dated him for a bit, so he obviously made her toes curl. I'd gathered enough details to know the relationship hadn't ended well. With Ruby's general disrespect for laws and rules, and her determination to live life on her own terms—which had included pot smoking, streaking, and many arrests—it wasn't a surprise a relationship with a sheriff had fizzled.

What did he want? I briefly considered hiding behind the island in the kitchen until he meandered off. Instead, I decided to act like an adult and open the door.

"Bernadette," he said gruffly, tipping his cowboy hat.

"Gosh, I loved it when he talked like Clint Eastwood," Ruby sighed. "He used to do this thing with his handcuffs where—"

"What can I do for you, Sheriff?" I asked, having zero interest in the rest of Ruby's story.

"May I come in?"

I stepped aside. "Of course."

As I shut the door, he glanced around the entryway and living room. "How are things going, Bernie?"

"Everything's fine," I said, my brow creasing in worry. It wasn't every day the police showed up at my front door. Well, Adam, my boyfriend, came by often, of course. But never the sheriff. Except when I'd found a dead guy upstairs.

"We received a complaint of multiple cars parked out in front of your home last night and too much noise. I'm here to look into it."

Wait. *What?*

"I... I... have no idea what you're talking about."

He narrowed his gaze on me. "You sure about that? You sound a little guilty."

"Well, I'm definitely not guilty of anything," I replied. "Maybe what you hear is confusion."

"What happened here last night?"

"Nothing!"

"Did you have a big party?" the sheriff asked, placing his hands on his hips. "Like your crazy grandmother used to have?"

"Aww... poor Bruce is upset that I quit inviting him to mine," Ruby said, grinning. "If he hadn't been such a stick-in-the-mud, I'd have welcomed him with open arms. Instead, he blathered on about noise variances, illegal drugs, and indecent exposure."

"No, I didn't," I said, fisting my hands at my sides. "I was home alone." With my dead grandmother. But he didn't need to hear that part.

"Not according to your neighbor." He pulled out a small, spiral-bound notebook from his back pocket and flipped through the pages. "She said there had to be at least thirty people at your house and just as many cars." He slapped it closed and stared at me.

"It was just me, Sheriff. I don't know which neighbor would make up such lies, but I'm sorry she's wasted your time."

Actually, I knew exactly who had it out for me: Sylvia.

Next, he retrieved his phone from the inside pocket of his jacket and scrolled through it. "She also sent this in."

Sounds of people screaming and laughing played, all obviously having a great time.

"It sounds like a rager," Ruby sighed. "Dang it. I could only wish you'd have a party that big."

My jaw dropped as I listened. Sylvia had promised me she'd have my bed and breakfast shut down, but I'd never imagined she'd sink to such depths with blatant lies.

"How many guests do you have staying here right now?" he asked.

"None! It's just me! All of my rooms are empty!"

"And how many were here last night? Because from the sound of this recording, it was far over the capacity allowed by the city."

Grinding my jaw, I stared at the man and tried not to lose my temper.

"Better watch it or you're going to break a tooth," Ruby muttered.

"There was no one here but me last night," I said quietly. "Sylvia is lying to you because she wants my bed and breakfast closed. She made that very clear to me when she moved in."

"Why in the world would she want that?"

"You'd have to ask her," I muttered. "She lives across the street in the blue house."

The sheriff sighed and rubbed his eyes with his forefinger and thumb. "Here's the deal, Bernie. It's always best to solve your neighborhood disputes without police involvement.

Maybe you two should sit down and discuss everything."

I shook my head. "No, thanks."

"Well, if there are any future complaints about parties over here, we'll have to do a more thorough check and discuss yanking your licenses for overcrowding. You know the city is very particular about those things."

"I'm going to kill her," I muttered, ready to punch someone.

"Excuse me?"

I glanced up at the sheriff and grinned. "You're right. I do need to sit down with her and work out our grievances. I'll do my best to smooth this over."

Walker smiled and nodded. "Good girl. As you know, the sheriff's office has far more important things to do than deal with petty neighborhood disputes."

Condescending, sexist jerk. "Of course."

"Have a great afternoon, Bernie," he said, smiling and tipping his cowboy hat to me once again.

"Bye, bye, Bruce-y!" Ruby called while he sauntered down my walkway to his cruiser. Once he pulled away, I glanced at Sylvia's house and noted the front window blinds moving. "Hope you enjoyed the show," I muttered, then gave the house the one-fingered salute.

"So, what's next on the agenda?" Ruby asked. "This day isn't nearly as boring as I'd feared it would be!"

"We're going to Yolanda's neighborhood meeting," I grumbled. "We need to get rid of Sylvia."

I ARRIVED at Yolanda's a few minutes before four. Even though I'd lived kitty corner from her for three years, I hadn't spoken to her until the Christmas that just passed where Ruby had convinced me to make soap baskets for my neighbors as a present and to introduce myself.

In her fifties and fitter than I could ever hope to be, Yolanda beamed as she answered the door. She wore her black curly hair close to her scalp, her dark skin gleaming in what was left of the winter sunlight.

"Bernie! I'm so glad you could be here," she said, stepping aside. "Come on in. You're the first one to arrive."

Was that a bad or good thing? I hated being

late, but I also understood others disliked when people arrived early. Had I hit the sweet spot on arrival etiquette or was my timing off?

"Would you like some tea?" Yolanda asked with a smile, not upset in the least. As she led me from the entryway to the living room, I sighed with relief—I hadn't offended her with my early arrival. An interesting décor of blue and gold greeted me, as well as at least two dozen plants perched on tables, the windowsill, and hanging from the ceiling. As I sat on the ocean-colored couch, Ruby yelled, "No! Don't drink the tea! She used to serve it to me claiming it was good for me! It tastes like moldy woodchips!"

Duly noted. "No, thank you," I replied. "But a glass of water would be great."

Ruby settled in next to me as Yolanda headed for the kitchen. "Every time I came over here, she'd give me some of that tea. I'd always dump it in the plants when she wasn't looking. Nasty stuff."

"I don't know... it seems to be working wonders for her," I whispered. She didn't look a day older than thirty.

"Here you go," Yolanda said. After handing me my glass of water, she sank into the cushion on the opposite end of the couch and grinned.

"I love all your plants," I said. "The air seems just a bit fresher in here than outside."

"Yes. I love the pure oxygen they produce. Some of them flower, which is always pretty."

After taking a quick drink, I set my glass down on a coaster on top of the side table. "Who else is going to be here?"

Yolanda shook her head. "I invited everyone on the street. We'll see who's had enough of Sylvia and her antics. For me, she can't leave fast enough. I'll buy her dang house if I need to."

"Seriously?"

"LaLa always means business," Ruby said. "Shoot, I missed this lady."

"Well, if I could afford it, I would," Yolanda said. "Maybe I'll ask what she wants for it and take out a mortgage on this house."

"What's she done to you?" I asked, truly surprised Yolanda would go to such lengths to oust our neighbor.

"Come here," she said, standing. "Let's go to the back door."

I followed her through the living room jungle into the kitchen and dining room area. We stood at the sliding back door leading to the backyard. I gasped as I took in the beauty and tried to fathom Yolanda's water bill.

Grass stretched from one side to the other. Six-foot-high brick walls enclosed the area. Rose bushes and vines lined the back wall, all healthy and thriving. Potted plants framed the patio where a lounger and small couch sat in the shade.

On the left fence line stood four old lemon trees reaching about fifteen feet high. Their leaves and branches intermingled with each other, making for another barrier between Yolanda and Sylvia's yard.

"This is beautiful," I murmured. My yearly petunia planting seemed very weak in comparison to Yolanda's foliage game. The time she must spend tending to it all...

"Thank you, but here's what I wanted to show you." She pointed at the lemon trees as we stood shoulder to shoulder. "There's no way to see into Sylvia's yard, right?"

I nodded.

"She's on my case about spending time in my secluded area in the buff."

"A girl after my own heart," Ruby said from behind us. "Naked is the only way to be."

It figured Ruby had been close with Yolanda while alive. They seemed to be kindred spirits. "But she can't see into your place."

"If she stands on a rock and peers through the

bottom branches of the lemon trees, she can. But, she has to make an effort. She said she's going to turn me in to the police for indecent exposure."

I snorted and shook my head. "She's literally trying to see into your yard, and then complaining about it?"

"Yes. You're correct."

We both glanced over our shoulders as the doorbell rang. When Yolanda went to answer it, I stared at the lemon trees once again. Had a branch just moved, or was I seeing things?

"Come on!" Ruby said. "Let's go see who's at the door! I'm loving this neighborhood excitement!"

I followed Yolanda. She opened the panel to reveal our neighbor, Pete.

"Oh, look! It's the tree guy!" Ruby said. "I wonder if he's come to commiserate about the new vermin in the neighborhood."

Sylvia had made me aware she'd been complaining about the tree in Pete's yard, a huge Palo Verde she was sure would be toppled during a monsoon and block the street. The Verde stood tall and strong in the yard, its branches reaching for the corners of the lot. It didn't look bad or seem like a danger to me. Come the spring and early summer when the tiny yellow flowers bloomed, it would be a different story. Not because of its size, but because of my allergies. Then, I'd walk around town wishing I had a chainsaw so I could destroy every last one of them.

"Hey, ladies!" he said.

When I'd delivered Pete's Black Walnut soap at Christmas, a scent Ruby had assured me all men love, he'd been kind and thankful for my offering. Working in construction had given him a perma-tan, a hard, lean physique, and hands as rough as steel wool.

"It's nice to see you again, Pete," Yolanda said as I waved. "You remember Bernie?"

"Of course. How's it going?"

"Good," I said, taking his outstretched palm in mine. "I'm glad I'm not the only one here with Sylvia issues."

Yolanda placed her hand on his shoulder. "Do you want some tea, Pete? Wilder made it for me."

"No, thanks. I'm not much of a tea guy."

"Water? Coffee?"

"I'll regret having it this late in the day, but a cup of coffee sounds great."

"Cream and sugar?"

"Yes, please."

As Yolanda hurried into the kitchen to get the

brew going, Pete and I sat down. "It's horrible we have to have a meeting about Sylvia," he said. "But she's driving me crazy."

"Same here!" I told him a brief version of my encounter with the sheriff. "I wasn't going to come to this meeting, but after that, I figured I was either going to kill her or we'd come together and form a plan."

Pete chuckled and shook his head. "She's called the city on my tree, if you can believe that. Does it bother you? Be honest with me."

I shook my head. "Not at all. During the spring when it blooms, that'll be another story. I'm allergic."

"I've been meaning to cut it back, but working in construction, I've been so busy. Twelve-hour days, six days a week. I'm not a young guy any-more, so it really wears on me."

"He can't be any older than forty," Ruby said, narrowing her gaze on him. "As far as I'm con-cerned, he's young. But I'm dead, so what do I know?"

"Then, when Sylvia started in on me, I began to intentionally put it off," Pete continued. "If she wasn't such a nag, I may have cut it back by now."

"Don't worry about your tree," Yolanda said, returning from the kitchen with a steaming mug and handing it to Pete. "Seriously. The only one that tree is bothering is Sylvia, and I have a feeling she wakes up every single day of her life looking to be irritated by someone or something."

"I'm glad to hear it's okay with both of you," Pete said. After taking a sip of his coffee, his brow furrowed.

"Sorry. No cream. All I had was organic goat milk."

"Ah, I see." He set it down on the coffee table.

"That's going to end up in a plant," Ruby muttered. "Did you know Yolanda was the only person I ever knew who drank goat milk?"

"Is anyone else is coming?" Pete asked.

Yolanda shook her head. "We'll wait a few more minutes and see."

Pete smiled and met my gaze. "By the way, I loved that soap you made me for Christmas, Bernie. It was really gentle on my hands, and I think it softened them up a bit, which I didn't think would be possible."

"I loved mine, too," Yolanda said. "It reminded me of the soap your grandmother used to make for me. How did you know I'm a shea butter woman?"

Smiling, I glanced over at Ruby. "Lucky guess,"

I said. "I'm glad you both liked it. When I have time, I'll make some more."

"That would be wonderful!" Yolanda said as a knock sounded on the front door. She stood and hurried over to open it. Wilder Riker brushed a hand down his chest-length, black beard and grinned.

"Join the party, Wilder!" Yolanda said, stepping aside.

"Thank you," he said, his voice quiet. He smiled as he met my gaze, then shook Pete's hand as they exchanged pleasantries.

In his thirties, I found Wilder unique and fascinating. Bald headed with one of the thickest, longest beards I'd ever seen, his disposition didn't match his looks. Tattoos peeked out from the neck of his long-sleeved green t-shirt, as well as from the hem of his jeans. His sandaled feet also bore inked designs. In my never-ending attempts to avoid judging people by their looks, I'd failed once again by pegging Wilder—as his name suggested—a wild child. Yet, he was one of the quietest, kindest, most sincere people I'd ever met.

"Would you like some tea?" Yolanda asked.

"I'd love some," he replied. I smiled as he lowered himself into a gold armchair. "It's nice to see everyone here."

"We've all had enough," Pete said, shaking his head.

"Agreed," Wilder replied. Steepling his fingers in front of his chest, he shook his head. "I'm a big believer in live and let live. She's threatened to close my business."

"Same here," I said. "What do you do?"

"I have an herbal shop I run out of my house." Wilder's soft, calm voice was almost difficult to hear. "I make teas and salves. I'm not sure how she found out, but she did."

"She saw me leaving your home with my bag of tea leaves," Yolanda said, returning with another steaming cup. "She asked me what it was and I shared your amazing apothecary with her. I was trying to be nice, but it backfired for you, Wilder. That one's on me."

He shrugged and took the cup. "Is this the blood cleanser tea?"

Yolanda nodded.

"I can smell that garbage from here," Ruby said. "Resembles moldy, dirty socks."

How Ruby knew how to pinpoint that odor, I didn't want to know.

We all turned to the front door when another knock sounded. Tina Everly strode in with a grin, a wave, and a box of donuts. In her sixties, her skin resembled brown leather from spending so much time in the Arizona sun tending to her vegetable gardens. She wore her salt and pepper hair in a pixie cut. "Hello, neighbors!" she chirped. "Oh, that coffee smells wonderful!"

"Let me grab you a cup," Yolanda said. After a minute, she returned with a mug for Tina and a dining room chair. I sat on my side of the couch and we all huddled around the coffee table as Tina opened the pink box of goodies.

"Get the chocolate," Ruby urged.

I grabbed the glazed with strawberry filling.

"The chocolate would have been better. Maybe eat that one next? Let me live vicariously through you?"

No, only one donut. Ruby moaned when Wilder grabbed the chocolate.

"Let's get this meeting started," Yolanda said. I'd noticed she'd foregone the donut, which didn't surprise me. A woman didn't get to look like Yolanda by eating bakery treats. "We've got a problem in this neighborhood, and her name's Sylvia. For some of us, she's simply a thorn in our sides. For others, she's threatened livelihoods. Our lives were a lot more peaceful before she moved in, and I'm not sure what to do about her at this point."

"I think we've all tried being nice to her," Wilder said. "I offered her some teas I'd made, and she said she believed in medical science, not herbal witchcraft."

"Listen, there's something everyone here should know," Pete said. "I had an affair with Sylvia last year."

CHAPTER 3

Wait. What?!

Ruby squealed and spun around in a circle, her purple muumuu billowing out from her thin frame. "Oh! This is going to get good!"

I glanced around the room and found a couple of unhinged jaws to match my own.

"I'm sorry," Tina said. A donut sprinkle had stuck to her lip, falling to her lap as she spoke. "Could you repeat that? I don't think I heard you correctly."

Pete chuckled and shook his head. "Trust me, you did. I had an affair with Sylvia last year. I had no idea she was married at the time. It didn't end well."

My mind spun as I stared at my neighbor.

This sounded like a thriller film where someone ends up with a dead animal in a pot on their stove. "You had a relationship with her that ended badly and now she's moved into the same neighborhood as you? Did she know where you lived?"

"No. We always hooked up in a hotel room, usually in Cottonwood. She'd never been to my house."

"I can't imagine your surprise when you met your new neighbor," Yolanda said, laughing.

Pete smirked and snorted. "You have no idea. It would have been funny if it was anyone but her."

"And now she hounds you about the tree," Wilder said. "Was she shocked to see you as well?"

Pete tilted his head and studied the ceiling for a moment. "Now that I think about it, not really."

"Do you believe she moved to the neighborhood knowing you lived here?" Wilder asked, leaning forward, and placing his elbows on his knees.

"That would be creepy," Pete said. "I don't like to think about that."

I nodded in agreement. "Very stalkerish."

"It's something to consider," Yolanda said, turning to Tina. "You and I haven't spoken in a while, but I figured if Sylvia was bothering everyone else, she had to be getting to you, too. Now you're here, so I must have been right. What's up?"

Tina rolled her eyes. "She hates the vegetable garden in my front yard. Says it looks like a bunch of weeds. By the way, I've got a bumper crop of tomatoes if anyone's interested."

"I'll take some," Yolanda said. "I love tomatoes."

We all agreed to relieve Tina of some of her crop.

My neighbor had devoted her whole front yard to her vegetable garden. Raised beds made with railroad ties had been built, mostly by Tina. I'd seen a man helping her once or twice, but she swung the hammer and erected almost everything herself.

"But she saw your gardens before she bought the house," Yolanda said. "She knew they were there when she moved in."

Tina shrugged. "I'm not sure what to tell you. She's asked me to move them into the backyard. I didn't bother to inform her that is packed full as well."

"What do you do with what you harvest?" Wilder asked. "You can't possibly eat all the food you grow in your front yard, let alone everything in the back."

"I can some of it, make soups and donate a good portion of it to the local food banks. Everyone needs to eat their vegetables!"

"How lovely of you," Yolanda said. The rest of us nodded in agreement. "I had no idea, Tina."

"It's my pet project. I want to feed those in need. Once, not too long ago, I couldn't afford to eat healthy, so now I want to make sure that doesn't happen to others."

"You better step up your charity game," Ruby said. "Compared to Tina, you suck."

Wasn't that the truth. Time and money were my biggest enemies—I didn't have a lot of either.

"Now that we've established we're a pretty cool group of decent people, what are we going to do about Sylvia?" Yolanda asked.

Wilder shook his head. Pete shrugged. "You could stab her tires," Ruby offered.

Not helpful.

"Does anyone have any suggestions?" Yolanda asked, glancing at each of us. I decided not to offer Ruby's.

"Oh! I know!" Ruby yelled. "You could all break into her house in the middle of the night and hold her at knifepoint until she agrees to move! Of course, you'd be wearing masks and she'd never guess who you are!"

Glancing at my ghost, I bit my tongue. Where in the world did she get these ideas?

Ruby threw up her hands in exasperation. "Just tell her to go sit on the sun! She'll get the point that she's not wanted."

"I think the best thing for us to do is speak to her first," Tina said. The plan sounded reasonable to me. Much better than involving a weapon.

"That's the dumbest thing I've ever heard," Ruby muttered. "You don't get through to someone like Sylvia with civilized conversation."

"Which one of us should approach her?" Yolanda asked.

"Not me," Pete said. He held his hands out in front of him. "I'm trying to avoid her."

"I'm not very good with confrontation," Wilder said quietly, cradling his mug of tea. "I prefer to live peacefully."

"We all do, Wilder," Ruby sighed. "We all do. That's exactly what we're trying to achieve, dummy."

Yolanda glanced at me and I shook my head. "I'm not good at confrontation, either. And I've already had words with Sylvia. I spend most of my time tracking her movements so I can avoid her."

Tina laughed and shook her head. "I'll do it. That crabby B-word doesn't scare me."

"You all are a bunch of chickens," Ruby said. "If I were alive, I'd have volunteered in a hot second to slash her tires."

"Well, it's settled," Yolanda said, slapping her hands on her thighs. "Do you want to head over right now?"

I glanced over my shoulder out the window and found Sylvia's driveway empty. "She's not there."

"That's okay," Tina replied. "I'll speak to her first thing in the morning."

"I feel much better that I'm not the only one being targeted," Wilder said. "Thank you for having us over."

We chatted a few more minutes about the wonderful weather, then Pete stood. "I've got an early start at work in the morning and still have some things to take care of before I head to bed."

"I'm guessing it isn't the tree in your yard?" I asked. He threw his head back and laughed while the others joined in.

"Good one, Bernie," Pete replied. "But nope. Not tonight. I've got a date with a beer on my porch and some relaxation time. I'll see you all later."

"I need to go as well," I said. "I've got a full house arriving tomorrow, and I need to make sure everything is set."

"You already did that!" Ruby yelled.

Which was correct, but I wanted to head home. I'd had enough socialization for the time being.

"You should pull out a bottle of tequila and get this shindig started!" Ruby said. "We can dance, drink and have one heck of a time!"

"Thanks for coming, Bernie," Yolanda said. "Hopefully, we'll soon restore law and order in our neighborhood."

I hugged Yolanda and smiled. "Without you having to buy her house."

"No kidding, girl. Let's hope it doesn't get to that point. But I am willing to look into that because there's no way I'm moving."

"Me neither." I loved my home and living in Sedona. Yes, the big house was hard to manage, but being my own boss was worth it. Besides, what would I do without all my friends? Adam? And now all my lovely neighbors I finally had come to know?

After saying goodbye, Ruby and I returned to our home.

"It's time for Magnum P.I. reruns!" Ruby squealed. "Come on, let's settle in."

As much as I loved Tom Selleck and the show, I had promised myself I'd go for a run. "It's my exercise time," I said. "I'm going to have to skip it, but I can turn on the television for you. Unless you wanted to come with me?" Ruby would never join me in anything that remotely resembled a workout.

She shook her head. "The only time you should run is if someone's chasing you."

"Well, I'm doing it for my health."

"Party pooper."

"I'll turn on the television for you."

Since Ruby couldn't move inanimate objects, I had to do everything for her. Most of the time, it didn't bother me. Other times, I felt like her unwilling personal assistant.

Once the theme song played, I hurried into my room and slipped into my leggings and sweatshirt before I changed my mind. If I didn't get moving, I'd end up on the couch right next to my ghost.

I hurried out the back door and did some light stretching before getting on my way. When I rounded my house onto the main street, I glanced up at Sylvia's. Pleased to find her car still absent, I took a deep breath and went on my way.

My feet pounded against the pavement, my heart rate increased, and soon, I found myself lost in thought.

Once I'd discovered Ruby's existence, my dedication to my health and fitness had taken a turn. Well, not even a turn. It had gone straight down the tubes and sat at the far end of my priority list. I adored Ruby, but her love of cop shows and sweets had rubbed off on me, bringing me to a level of laziness I'd never known. My New Year Resolution had been to start taking care of myself again, and so far, it was going well.

I rounded the corner just as the sun set behind the majestic red rocks. Total darkness was still a way away, so I'd make it home before then.

Since I used to run five miles with relative ease, I grew irritated when I started huffing and puffing at a mile and a half. By two miles, I was gasping for air with my hands on my knees. *Patience. You'll get back into shape.*

Hands on hips, I walked home. A two-mile run and a two-mile walk was nothing to sneeze at. As I turned the corner onto my street, relief once again swept through me when I noted

Sylvia's car was still gone. I waved at Pete, who sat on his front porch drinking a beer. My other neighbors could be seen moving about inside their homes while I walked by. A hammer and saw lay in Tina's front yard, and I debated whether to knock on her door and remind her she'd left them out but decided to mind my own business. No one in the neighborhood would steal her tools.

When I arrived at my house, I turned as head-lights shone behind me.

Sylvia.

She'd stopped in front of Pete's. He walked over to the passenger side and leaned over through the open window. I couldn't hear what was said, but by the volume and tone of Sylvia's voice, she was giving him an earful.

This was confirmed when Pete slammed the top of her car, and threw his beer can at her bumper. Pointing at her, he yelled, "I've had enough! Drop dead, Sylvia!"

He picked up his can and marched back to his house as she drove toward me. Oh, no. I sprinted behind my house and opened the back door, then slammed it shut. Hurrying to the front windows, I peeked through the blinds as Sylvia exited her vehicle and marched into her home. I sighed and stepped away when her lights went on.

Ruby stood right behind me. "What are you doing?" she asked as I gasped.

"Don't scare me like that!"

She smiled and pointed at the blinds. "Are you spying on Sylvia again?"

I placed my hand over my heart and tried to catch my breath. "Yes. She and Pete just got into a big fight."

"Over what? His tree? If that's the case, she's got some deep-seated issues with that poor Palo Verde."

"I don't know what the argument was over. All I heard was Pete telling her to drop dead."

Ruby shrugged and nodded. "That may not be a bad idea. She should take his advice."

"That's not very nice."

"Just call 'em as I see 'em, Bernie."

CHAPTER 4

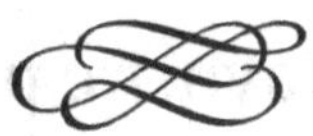

I WOKE the next morning bright and early, ready to take on the day. Planting petunias in my planters leading up to the front door would be my first task immediately after a little yoga and some coffee.

And some Advil. My attempts to get back into shape had my legs feeling as if they'd met the business end of a baseball bat. Even though I'd been at it about a month, the pain didn't seem to ease up.

"When do we get to see Ned?" Ruby asked.

"I'm not sure," I replied, sipping my coffee. "I've got to talk to Adam. I thought he would've called last night, but I didn't hear from him."

Ned, the ghost who lived with Adam, had informed me that he would appreciate it if I didn't bring Ruby around so much. As a cowboy from a century ago, he preferred the quiet life, and having Ruby around was anything but that. However, I didn't have the heart to tell Ruby. Teasing Ned was one of her favorite pastimes.

"It's been at least a week since I've been over there," Ruby complained. "Maybe we can go today?"

"Nope." I set my mug into the sink and headed for the front door. "I've got guests checking in. We don't have time."

Ruby trailed behind me, cursing and complaining, as we exited the house. Sylvia's car was in the driveway, her garage open. Taking a deep breath, I was determined to get the flowers in the soil and not hide from her. The neighborhood was on my side. Our army of five was strong.

I grabbed my gloves and the petunias I'd purchased from the shed. I carried everything around to the front, glad I'd slipped on my sweatshirt. In a couple of hours, I wouldn't need it, but a chill still hung in the fresh, morning air.

Ruby stretched out face up on the walkway, her hands laced behind her head. As I slowly squatted down to dig, my legs protested, and I groaned in pain. Maybe I needed to ease up on my plan of getting back into shape.

"All that running isn't good for you," Ruby said, closing her eyes. "I told you, the only time you should run is if someone's chasing you. Your knees will go out early."

Ignoring her, I pushed my shovel into the dirt and dug my hole. Being outside in the fresh air lifted my spirits and I found myself humming and appreciating the time alone before my guests arrived.

After the first pot had been filled with the red, pink, and purple flowers, Ruby said, "I wish I could feel the sun on my face. I always loved that."

And she also wished she could drink tequila, be heard by anyone but me and Ned, laugh with her friends, and turn on the television herself. I sighed with pity. Would she ever find her final resting place, or would she be trapped here forever?

I glanced over at Sylvia's—still no action. With her garage door up, I expected her to emerge from her home at any time.

Tina walked out into the street and waved at me as she headed towards Sylvia's.

"It's go-time," Ruby said, sitting up. "Hope

she's armed for her confrontation with Satan's sister."

I turned back to my next barrel as Tina knocked on Sylvia's door, the sound echoing across the street. Ruby kept me in the loop with a running commentary. "Sylvia's not answering. Tina's knocking again. Still no answer. I wonder what Sylvia's doing? Maybe she's on the toilet? In the shower? I would think she'd answer the dang door. Now Tina's walking over to the garage. Maybe Sylvia's out back? That's weird, her garage door is open."

An ear-shattering scream scared me so badly, I scrambled on my hands and knees toward my house.

"Hurry up!" Ruby yelled as she stood. "It's Armageddon across the street!"

The pain in my legs now forgotten, I scrambled to my feet and rushed across the pavement and past Sylvia's car. I found Tina hunched over Sylvia, who lay in the middle of her garage wearing her blue hospital scrubs, spread-eagle. In fact, her pose reminded me of a star. A hammer lay next to her while blood pooled around her head like a halo. Her pale blue eyes stared upward, devoid of any life.

"Bernie! Call someone!" Tina yelled hysterically. "I think she's dead!"

"Uh oh," Ruby muttered. "Someone nixed the neighbor."

I pulled my phone out of my back pocket and dialed 9-1-1 with shaky hands.

"Better tell her to step away from the body," Ruby said. "She's going to get tears and snot all over the crime scene."

Crime scene? Well, unless Sylvia had hit herself in the head with a hammer hard enough to make herself bleed, Ruby was right.

I stepped forward and grabbed Tina by the bicep. "Come sit outside," I urged just as the operator answered.

Tina followed me to the front porch and plopped down on a chair. "We need an ambulance," I said, giving Sylvia's address. "I think... someone's dead." I turned back to Tina. "Right? She's dead?"

Tina stared off into space, her body trembling as she nodded.

"She's dead," I said again. "Please... send someone."

I glanced back at the garage and then at Tina. According to her, there was nothing to be done for Sylvia. However, the way Tina shook and cried, I was afraid she was going to have a nervous breakdown and there'd be another prone body on the property. Sitting next to her, I took her palm in mine. "It's okay," I said, trying to keep my voice even. She stared at our intertwined hands as if they were a foreign entity.

"I think she was killed," Tina whispered. "The hammer… the blood…"

"Does she think she pounded her own skull?" Ruby asked, snorting. "Of course, she was murdered! Another mystery to be solved, Bernie! Isn't it exciting?"

With a deep breath, I focused on Tina and not my callous grandmother. "You're probably right. The police will be here soon."

"I'm all of a sudden quite cold," Tina whispered, running her hands over her arms. Noticeable goosebumps crawled over her flesh. Possible shock?

After pulling off my sweatshirt, I handed it to her. "Put this on. Or at least wrap it around your shoulders."

She took it and held it to her chest as sirens wailed in the distance.

A police cruiser pulled up and Adam jumped from the car and ran up the walk. Relief flooded his features as I stood and he took me in his arms.

"I'm so glad to see you," he whispered. "When I heard a body had been found on your street, I panicked."

I wrapped my arms around his waist and allowed myself to be comforted for a moment before he had to get down to business. "I'm fine," I whispered. "Sylvia isn't."

He held me at arm's length. "Where is she?"

"In the garage." Hitching my thumb over my shoulder, I whispered, "Tina found her. I think she may be in shock."

Adam nodded and squatted down in front of Tina. "Are you going to be okay?"

She stared at him wordlessly. As he glanced up at me, I only worried for my neighbor more. It appeared she was shutting down.

"The ambulance will be here soon, and I'd like them to take a look at you," Adam said. "Is that going to be okay?"

Finally, she nodded, and I sighed in relief. At least she was somewhat responsive. Adam stood, returned to me, and kissed the top of my head. "Please stay here with her. I'm going to look in the garage."

I sat next to Tina again and took her hand. Ruby plopped down on the porch in front of us and stretched her legs out in front of her. "What a morning," she said. "Another dead body. Who do you think did it?"

Unable to answer because I didn't talk to my ghost in public, I simply shrugged.

"Do you think it was Tina?" Ruby asked.

I glanced over at the distraught woman whose hand trembled in mine. If so, she was one heck of an actress. I shook my head.

The ambulance arrived, as did the sheriff himself. My end of the street was now blocked with emergency vehicles.

"Let's go say hello to Brucey Boy," Ruby said as he hurried into the garage, the EMTs on his heels.

I wasn't going to leave Tina, and I doubted the sheriff wanted us back in the crime scene, so I stayed put.

Yolanda, Pete, and Wilder strode up the sidewalk as one of the EMTs hurried over to Tina and me. He squatted down in front of her and smiled, his gaze roaming her face.

"He's going to make sure you're okay," I said, squeezing Tina's hand, then letting it go. I walked down the path to the rest of my neighbors.

"What's going on?" Wilder asked.

"Sylvia's dead," I said. "I think she was murdered."

The three stared at me wide eyed. "Oh, my goodness," Yolanda whispered. "How awful."

"Dang it," Pete muttered, scrubbing a hand over his face. "That's horrible."

Wilder simply turned to the house, then crossed his arms over his chest.

"Tina found her," I continued. "She's really upset."

"That's understandable," Yolanda said. "Should someone go sit with her?"

I glanced behind me and saw the EMT taking her blood pressure. "Maybe in a bit. Let them finish and make sure she's okay."

The four of us gazed at Sylvia's garage in silence. Ruby had been right. Unless she'd knocked herself over the head with a hammer, she'd been killed by someone. But by whom?

I glanced at my neighbors. All of us had tangled with the woman. Like me, she'd threatened to shut down Wilder's herb business. She and Yolanda had argued and fought over Yolanda's preference of nudity in her backyard. Pete had an affair with her and she'd been hassling him about trimming his tree.

Recalling what I'd witnessed the previous evening after my run, I studied him a little closer. *Drop dead, Sylvia.* Perhaps he'd helped her along?

A car pulled up behind the ambulance and sheriff's vehicles. A family gaped at the scene and I realized they were probably my guests. With a curse, I hurried over while running a hand over my hair and pasting a smile on my face. The driver rolled down his window.

"Hi, there!" I said, my voice as chipper as I could make it. "Are you checking in?"

"What's going on here?" the woman in the passenger seat asked.

The man glanced over at Sylvia's again. "Yes. What's happening?"

"Oh, nothing," I said. "Let's get you checked in. The bed and breakfast is right over here."

They continued to stare at Sylvia's house, and I pursed my lips. How in the world did I get their attention away from the calamity across the street? I needed them inside my house, handing me a credit card.

"Doesn't seem like the looky-loos are going to budge anytime soon," Ruby muttered.

"I'm not sure about this, Ralph," the woman said. She leaned over her husband and glanced up at me. "Are you sure you don't know what's going on there?"

"She's… my neighbor's sick," I said. "Come on into the house. We'll get you checked in."

It wasn't *exactly* a lie. Tina was in shock or something, so yes, she was ill. I'd just left out the details of the dead woman in the garage.

Just when I thought I'd had them convinced, the sheriff strode out of the garage and waved me over. "Get over here, Bernadette," he shouted. "This is a murder investigation, and we need to speak to you."

"Murder!" the husband and wife yelled in unison. They quickly exchanged glances as my hopes of keeping them as customers vanished.

"I think we need to find somewhere else to stay," he said, throwing the gearshift in reverse. "Honey, call the others and tell them what's going on. This isn't a safe neighborhood."

The wife pulled out her cell phone while he backed up and executed a three-point turn. As they drove away, a sinking feeling settled in the pit of my stomach. My bank account needed those reservations.

"Welp, you got what you wanted," Ruby said.

"What does that mean?"

"Sylvia's out of your hair."

"I never wanted her dead," I muttered.

"But she's no longer a part of the neighborhood, so that's good." Ruby tapped on her lip and shook her head. "Even though she's dead, she succeeded."

"In what?"

"Burning down your business... not literally, but figuratively. Your rooms are empty, just the way she wanted it."

CHAPTER 5

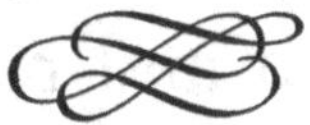

WHEN THE LOCAL PRESS ARRIVED, the sheriff shooed my neighbors and me all back to our homes with a promise that he'd be by to speak to everyone who lived on the street. Ruby and I sat in the living room staring into space, her hand moving over the back of my cranky tabby, Elvira. Sure, I felt awful Sylvia was dead. Perhaps I should be more upset, more in line with Tina's reaction. However, I'd discovered dead people before. Was I used to it? Of course not. I couldn't imagine a time when finding a body wouldn't upset me. But I also didn't require medical care. Once the initial shock wore off, I'd be over finding Sylvia. Cold, I know, but the woman had tried to take away my livelihood, so I most likely wouldn't shed a tear over her demise.

My other mounting problems? Now those had my panties in a knot, as Ruby would say, and my stress level slowly rose. It continued to creep up as I sat on the couch and realized how dire my financial situation had become. I wanted to toss my cookies.

Three rooms full for a week was a huge chunk of money to lose out on and my heart thundered with panic. What if I couldn't pay my power bill? Thankfully, I didn't have a mortgage, but I did have a tax bill coming due. I'd been counting on that money to pay it.

"So, what do we do now?" Ruby said. "I have an idea! We can go visit Ned!"

"We're waiting here," I replied. "The sheriff is going to want to speak to me and right now I'm on the verge of a panic attack as I try to figure out how I'm going to pay that tax bill."

"You should've had your business restructured like I suggested."

"I tried. The lawyer ended up dead, remember?"

Ruby shrugged. "Find a new one."

Of course, she was right. But the issue had been relegated to the back burner as the holidays had approached, not to mention my newly rekindled romance with Adam. Hanging out with him had been much more important than finding a breathing lawyer who knew something about taxes and business structure.

However, my predicament had now moved to the top of my list of important things I could no longer ignore.

To work off some of my nervous energy, I paced in front of my fireplace with my ghost and cat watching every step.

When the doorbell rang, I hurried over and flung it open. Sheriff Bruce Walker stood before me, the TV crew filming him from the street.

"Ms. Maxwell," he said, his voice gruff. "May I come in?"

I stepped aside and stared at the floor hoping I would somehow become invisible to the press. Once he'd crossed the threshold, I slammed the door.

"Well, hello, sheriff," Ruby purred as she circled him. "How lovely to see you again."

"It's crazy how this house still smells like Ruby," he muttered while his nose twitched. With her only inches away from him, the scent of lavender and marijuana had to be overpowering.

"Do you want to sit down?" I asked, pointing

toward the living room. "Can I get you a glass of water or something?"

He shook his head as he passed me. "I'm here on business." Elvira meowed and ran when he entered. I wished I could follow because I didn't want to relive my morning. In fact, going back to bed and starting over sounded like an excellent plan.

Ruby sat down next to him as he settled into the couch across from me. "Tell me what happened this morning," he demanded while he took off his cowboy hat and set it on the side table. He stared at me while he ran his hand over his thick gray hair.

"I used to love to run my fingers through that mop," Ruby said. She reached up and did just that. "Bruce liked it, too."

He glanced around the living room. "I feel a slight draft."

"Sorry about that," I muttered, glaring at my ghost. People often experienced a cold blast of air when she was near. "But getting back to your question, this morning I was planting petunias out front when I saw Tina walking over to Sylvia's. A few moments later, she started screaming. I ran over and found her hunched over the body, quite upset."

He pulled out a notebook from his breast pocket and began writing. "What time was that?"

"Maybe seven? Eight? I didn't look at the clock."

"Tell me about Tina."

I shrugged. "What about her?"

"She's your neighbor." He narrowed his gaze as if he thought I was the dumbest person on the planet. "What do you know about her?"

Up until recently, she was the woman in her sixties who I waved at when I saw her tending to her gardens. Now, she was my fellow warrior, banded together with the others to put a stop to a woman's threats and antics. Who just now happened to be dead.

Someone had succeeded in ending her neighborhood tyranny. But had it been Tina?

"She grows a lot of food and gives it to the soup kitchens and homeless shelters," I blurted. "She's got a bumper crop of tomatoes right now." Beyond that, I really didn't know what else to say. Some may find it strange that I could live in a house for three years and not have better knowledge of my neighbor. To me, being somewhat introverted, it was perfectly acceptable. "Is she okay?"

"They took her to the hospital for observation," he replied. "Her blood pressure was high."

"How long will she be there?" I should go visit just to be supportive.

"I'm not sure. Let's get back to the mess across the street. Once you found Tina and Sylvia, what happened next?"

"Well, I realized that Sylvia had most likely been murdered and we were standing in the middle of a crime scene, so I helped her out to the front porch and dialed 9-1-1."

"And you knew she was murdered... how?"

Ruby snorted as I tried not to roll my eyes. Stupid question for the win. "I just sort of guessed. There was a hammer, blood around her head... I assumed someone had hit her with it."

The sheriff nodded while taking more notes. "Tell me about your relationship with the victim."

I sighed and rubbed my temples. Yes, returning to bed sounded better and better with each minute ticking by. "We had our disagreements. She wanted to shut down my bed and breakfast. She made all sorts of false claims, like the big party you were out here investigating the other day. There was never a party. She told me the day she moved in that she would be actively trying to close my place of business."

"Not very neighborly," he muttered.

"No. She also hassled the others on the street, but you can ask them about it."

"Give me some examples."

I almost blurted that Sylvia also wanted to close Wilder's business, but I wasn't sure if his was legal. Skip his drama. Would Yolanda want the sheriff to be aware she liked to enjoy her private Garden of Eden in the nude? I didn't want to embarrass her by contributing the information, just in case. And Pete... well, she'd hassled him about the stupid tree. Tina, her gardens. Those seemed safe to discuss, which I did in detail.

"Have any of your neighbors made threats against the victim?"

Yes, but should I share what I witnessed the previous night between her and Pete? It felt a little traitorous, like I was turning on my fellow comrade in arms. It was one thing to speak about the Palo Verde, and quite another to discuss a failed affair that ended badly. I shook my head. "We all wanted to be left alone, and she made it difficult to live here. But I can promise you, no one wanted to see her dead."

The sheriff eyed me a long moment, then said, "You did."

Dread settled in my gut. "Excuse me?"

"You said you wanted her dead when I was here about the party complaint. I even wrote it down in my notebook." He flipped back a few pages. "You said, and I quote, 'I'll kill her.'"

I swallowed the bile rising in my throat. "It... it was a figure of speech. I would never wish anyone dead."

"Well, Bernie," Ruby said as she ran her hand over the sheriff's hair again, "you've got yourself in a pickle. Brucey boy has you in his sights."

Biting my lip, I didn't respond to Ruby, but to Walker I said, "I didn't mean I wanted to literally kill her. She was lying about me, and she'd threatened to have my business closed. What I meant was that I was really upset and angry."

"Angry enough to kill her?"

"No! Of course not!" My stomach roiled and my coffee threatened to make another appearance.

"We'll see about that," he muttered as he wrote in his notebook. "I'm not sure where that draft is coming from, but you better have that looked into. And it's a good thing marijuana is now legal, or I'd arrest you for drugs."

Tears welled in my eyes as Ruby blew in his ear again. Sometimes I swore my ghost liked to see me in trouble just because she liked the drama and action. A knock sounded at the front door and as I stood to answer it, Adam hurried in.

"They're a bunch of dang vultures out there," he said, hitching his thumb over his shoulder at the press. "Everything okay in here?"

His face fell when our gazes met.

"I'll let her tell you all about it," the sheriff said, standing. "But your girlfriend's in a bit of a bind. You may want to inform her that our office takes threats to kill people very seriously."

Adam placed his hands on my shoulders and stared at me, remaining quiet until the front door closed. "What did that mean?"

"The other night when Sylvia called the sheriff about a party I supposedly had, he came out the next day. According to him, I said I was going to kill her."

His gaze widened. "You *what?*"

My tears finally tracked down my cheeks as the gravity of my situation settled. "It was a figure of speech. She's... she was so awful to me and everyone on the block. I didn't mean anything by it."

"I know you didn't," he replied, taking me in his arms. "I know."

"He thinks I may have had something to do with Sylvia dying, Adam, and that scares me."

Ruby sighed and rolled her eyes. "Would you please quit with the tears and drama?"

Stepping away from Adam, I swiped my wet cheeks and turned to my ghost. "Why do you have to be so difficult? Did you hear the sheriff? If marijuana wasn't legal, he'd arrest me... and all because you insisted on blowing in his ear and running your fingers through his hair! You couldn't keep your hands off him!"

"I used to date him!" Ruby yelled. "I promise you, he misses me! I was giving him a little reminder of how good things used to be!"

"You said it was the worst relationship of your life!"

Ruby shrugged. "It had its good moments. They were few and far between, but there were a couple."

"Okay, okay," Adam said, holding his hands up in front of him. "I can only hear one side of this conversation, but based on how upset Bernie is, it's an argument. Please stop. Let's just relax for a minute and get things figured out."

"The sheriff just told me that I'm a suspect in Sylvia's murder," I said. "There's nothing to figure out."

"Sure, there is!" Ruby said. "We'll find out who killed her and get you off the hook."

I repeated her words to Adam. He sighed and sat down on the couch, laying his head back against the cushions. "I don't like you involved in these things. Please stay out of it, especially since you threatened to kill your neighbor."

"Okay, I will," I said.

"Don't roll over so easily!" Ruby yelled. "If you want to solve this murder, let's do it."

But I didn't. I'd been interviewed by the sheriff himself. Certainly, he'd realized that investigating me further would be nothing but a waste of time. There was no way I was still on the suspect list.

Instead of playing Nancy Drew, I had to fire up my marketing machine and figure out how to get more people staying at my bed and breakfast. Hopefully, the news of the murder would die down quickly… or maybe I should use it to my advantage? There were people currently standing outside my door focused on Sylvia's house. Invite the press to stay? Ugh. No way. Maybe I could market my bed and breakfast as the place to stay to see a murder site?

How tacky, though. I hated the idea of profiting off someone's untimely death. However, she'd also been the one who wanted to close my doors.

In the meantime, I'd stay in my lane and leave the murder-solving to the professionals.

CHAPTER 6

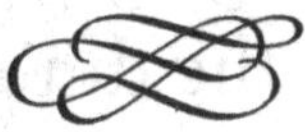

TWO HOURS LATER, I paced my big, empty house that was supposed to be teeming with people, trying to figure out how I could exit without being hounded by the press. The idea of using Sylvia's murder still played back and forth in my mind. *It's necessary! It's tacky! You could make some big money! You're benefitting from your neighbor's death. She wanted your business closed! That doesn't mean I should stoop to that level. How are you going to pay your tax bill?*

Granted, I'd never tried to squash the rumors that my bed and breakfast was haunted, even though I'd never believed it. So, in theory, I'd made money off Ruby's ghostly ways. That seemed different to me, though. Number one, I hadn't intentionally profited off her death. Second, she was my grandmother, not some surly stranger. And third, Ruby was actually haunting the house.

I heard my ghost giggling in the front entry, and I snuck through the dining room to see what she was up to. She was bent over at the window, her purple muumuu wrapped around her waist, mooning the news crews gathered outside. I stared at her for a long moment as she laughed and snorted while shaking her bottom. If she were alive, I doubted her actions would have been any different.

"Enjoying yourself?" I asked.

She glanced up and me and nodded. "Heck, yes. You want to join me and give them something to film?"

I shook my head and sighed.

Ruby stood upright and let her muumuu fall around her ankles. "By the way, Tina's home. Someone just dropped her off. She made it inside before the vultures ate her alive."

I walked over to the window and peered out. One television crew and a bunch of other people were milling about. Who were they? Probably the paper... perhaps a true crime blogger or two? People with an unhealthy obsession for murder?

In total, I counted fifteen camped out in front of my house.

My phone buzzed in my pocket, and I pulled it out to answer. Yolanda.

"Tina's home, Bernie," she said without preamble. "I tried to call, but there wasn't any answer. I think one of us should be there, but with this crowd of reporters out here, I'm afraid to cross the street."

"How can I get out of here without dealing with them?" I mused. I also wanted to check up on Tina.

"What about out the back?" Ruby said. "Cut across the lot and into the desert. If you stay low, they'll never spot you between the houses."

Because of the way my home was situated and the lot size, a lot of ground lay between Tina's and mine. If the press saw me attempting to make it to her place the back way, it wouldn't take much for them to catch me, especially if they didn't mind trespassing. As a man came halfway up my walkway, turned, and snapped a picture of Sylvia's home, encroaching on private property seemed to be a non-issue for them.

"You need a distraction," Ruby said. "I'd be happy to go streaking down the road, but they'd never see me."

And she wouldn't get too far with our tether outside the house in place. Not helpful.

"Since you were with her this morning, I think you should be the one to make sure she's okay," Yolanda said. "She'll want to talk about it with you. Share the experience. Stuff like that."

Was I interested in reliving it all? Not really. However, I was concerned about Tina.

"I'll go outside and act like I'm checking the mailbox," Yolanda said. "All their attention will be on me. Then, you can head over."

Yolanda was offering herself as the martyr, the sacrifice. That worked. Better her than me. "Sounds good. I'll go the back way just to make sure they don't spot me. Give me five minutes before you head out."

"You owe me," she grumbled.

What that consisted of, I had no idea, but I'd find out later. "Of course. Yes."

I hung up and hurried into my room and slipped on my black sweatshirt, then pulled the hood over my head.

"She's out in her driveway!" Ruby yelled, then raced into the kitchen before I reached the back door. "You aren't leaving me here!"

No argument from me. I didn't have time.

I crept outside and quietly shut the door behind me. As I tip-toed to the edge of the house, Ruby followed closely.

"Go look and see if Yolanda's still out there," I whispered.

Ruby rounded the corner and yelled obscenities, then mooned the reporters.

"Would you knock it off?" I hissed. "What are they doing?"

"They're chasing after LaLa," Ruby said, barely able to catch her breath through her cackling. "Let's go, Columbo!"

I kept my gaze focused on Tina's house and sprinted across the natural landscape, the sagebrush scraping against my jeans. When I reached Tina's fence, I realized I hadn't planned well. How was I supposed to scale a six-foot high brick wall?

"Jump it! Jump it!" Ruby yelled, her gaze still fixed on the reporters.

"I don't know how!"

Ruby turned to me and placed her hands on her hips. "What the heck's wrong with you? Didn't your mother ever show you how to climb a wall?"

"No!" I whispered. "It was never on my list of important things to learn." As a deeply conservative woman, my mother, Ruby's daughter, wouldn't have any need to jump a wall. She'd never find herself in any situation where it would be necessary.

"That's a shame," Ruby said. "Everyone should know how to scale a brick wall."

"What do I do?" I asked, glancing over my shoulder. Yolanda walked up her driveway wearing jeans and a tank top which flattered her ultra-fit body. The press surrounded her, and she yelled at them to get off her property before she called the police.

I did owe her. At least she looked fantastic for the cameras.

"The key is to run at it," Ruby said. "You run and keep your eyes at the highest point. Put a foot on the wall at the same time you grab the top. Then push with your feet and pull with your hands. It's easy!"

Furrowing my brow, I stared at the bricks. Being a hair under five foot five, it seemed huge to me. How in the world did I get my hands at the top and pull myself over?

With no time to give the semantics much more consideration, I ran at the wall, placed my foot against it and somehow hurled myself toward the top. To my utter surprise, my hand gripped the rough brick.

"Run up the wall!" Ruby yelled. "Move your feet like you're running! Pull with your arms!"

I did as instructed. My feet climbed while I grunted and groaned as my shoulders strained. The rough concrete dug into my hands and I hoped it didn't break any skin.

"That's my girl!" Ruby said. "You've got this!"

With one final push with my feet and pull with my hands, I was on top, and unfortunately, also on my way down. I landed on the other side with a thud, the breath leaving my lungs in one loud whoosh.

"Fantastic!" Ruby said. "But dang... you're lucky you didn't stake yourself."

I glanced to my left and found a large, wood pole right next to me. Rolling to my stomach, I realized I was in the middle of a garden. The overpowering smell of mint and basil engulfed me.

"Who are you and what are you doing in my backyard?"

Glancing over my shoulder, I found Tina standing a few feet away, training a gun on me. A bullet was the last thing I needed. "It's me, Bernie," I said, pulling off my hood and pushing my hair from my face. "I came to check on you, but the reporters out front are making it difficult."

Her shoulders sagged and she shook her head. "You scared me to death. I thought you were one of them."

Wincing, I struggled to my feet. Everything hurt, and I imagined it would only be worse tomorrow. "Yolanda tried to call you, but there wasn't any answer. We just wanted to know if you're okay."

Tina sighed and ran a hand over her salt and pepper pixie cut. "My phone's dead. Let's get you out of my herb garden," she said. "Come into the house."

I gently stepped around the plants and out of the planter while picking greenery out of my hair. Tina hadn't been lying when she said her backyard was just as packed as her front. Railroad tie planters had been built from one end to the other, most filled with different foliage.

"I've got carrots and squash over here," Tina said, pointing to her right. "To the left is the tomatoes. Let's make sure you take some home with you."

As I followed her into the house, I couldn't imagine the amount of work it took to keep up with it all. Her garden must be a full-time occupation for her.

We entered the house. As I closed the sliding glass door, she asked, "Do you want some lemonade? I made it with lemons from Yolanda's trees."

"I'd love some. Thank you."

As I sat down at the kitchen table, I studied the space. White cabinets, brown tiled flooring—simple, clean, and functional, just like Tina.

She brought over two glasses and sat down.

"Did everything go okay at the hospital?" I asked.

She nodded and smiled. "Yes. Finding Sylvia just spiked my blood pressure. They wanted to watch me for a few hours and let me go once everything had settled."

"I'm glad to hear that."

Her grin faded. "I'm going to be in a lot of trouble, Bernie."

I fought a grimace as I sipped my lemonade. A bit too much sugar for me. "Why is that?"

"That hammer we found by Sylvia?"

"What about it?"

"It was mine."

With a gasp, I set down my glass. "How do you know that?"

"I had some tools out front, one of them being

my hammer. The rubber grip is coming apart and there's a chunk of it missing. My hammer killed her."

When I came home from my run, I had noticed the tools and wondered if I should mention they'd been left out. "You're certain?"

She nodded. "That morning, when I headed out to see Sylvia, I saw it was gone. I remembered leaving it outside, but then figured I'd picked it up or misplaced it. Then there it was, next to Sylvia."

"Or perhaps she grabbed it and went over and knocked Sylvia's brains out," Ruby said. "She could have been hiding it in her jacket, or even carrying it down by her leg. You never would have seen it."

Good point. But was the woman in her sixties sitting across from me a killer? I didn't think so.

"What do you think happened?" I asked. "Someone on their way to see Sylvia picked up the hammer from your yard?"

She shrugged and shook her head. "They must have. I didn't kill her, although the cops are going to find my fingerprints on the hammer."

"You don't know that. Maybe the killer wiped it down to hide their own prints."

"Except, I picked it up to look at it when I

found Sylvia to make sure it was mine. I wasn't thinking."

I stared at my neighbor. She'd come upon a body and picked up the hammer that had most likely been used to kill?

"Did you tell the cops that?" I asked.

"No. I haven't had my formal statement taken yet."

The sheriff's office was going to have a field day with Tina's mistake, and they'd dig to make sure she wasn't lying about it. On one hand, maybe it would take the target off me. On the other, her life would become more difficult than she could probably imagine.

With a sigh, I smiled, hoping to hide the fact that I believed she was in deep doodoo—even more so than me. A stupid, flippant comment versus fingerprints on the murder weapon? Hands down, the cops should be more interested in the latter.

We chatted a few more minutes, then she grabbed a paper grocery bag and insisted on us going out to pick tomatoes. Once I had my bounty, she also tossed in a few onions. Maybe I could talk Darla, my friend and chef extraordinaire, into making me some salsa.

Thankfully, I didn't have to scale the wall to

return home, either. Tina pulled out a ladder from her shed and I climbed over easily. When I reached the top, I slowly lowered myself to the ground. Tina hurried up the ladder and handed me my bag. "See you later, Bernie!"

I waved and headed back to my house. With my dark sweatshirt and the night settling in, the remaining press either didn't see me, or decided I wasn't worth chasing.

Ruby and I settled in for the night with some Cagney and Lacey reruns.

"I think she did it," Ruby said when we were about halfway through the show. "I've been sitting here thinking about it, and sweet Tina had the motive, access to the murder weapon, and the opportunity to off Sylvia."

"You're wrong," I said, shaking my head. "She was too upset. They took her to the hospital for high blood pressure."

"That can be faked," Ruby said. "She just needed to get herself all worked up into a frenzy and her blood pressure would go up."

I'd never heard of such a thing.

"By the look on your face, you think I'm crazy," Ruby said. "Didn't you ever give yourself a fever so you could stay home from school when you were young?"

"No. That's ridiculous."

"What? Giving yourself a fever or wanting to stay home from school?"

It wouldn't have mattered. My mother would've given me some Tylenol and sent me whether my fever was real or not. I missed three days from kindergarten through high school. I even won an award for my excellent attendance record. "Mom didn't care about fevers," I grumbled. "I had to be throwing up in order skip class."

"Jeez, your mother is something else," Ruby muttered.

I stared at the television. Ruby's relationship with my mother hadn't really been given a chance to flourish since Ruby's parents took her away almost directly after birth, claiming Ruby wasn't fit to be a mother. Whether that was true or not, she wasn't allowed to discover.

Ruby sighed. "But getting back to the dead lady across the street, the police are going to be a bee in Tina's bonnet. I mean, who makes a mistake like that? Touching a murder weapon? My guess is she offed Tina, had her hissy fit for the cops' sake, then realized her mistake while she was in the hospital. She came up with the story and is now acting all worried."

Ruby wasn't wrong. Tina could've grabbed the

hammer on her way to Sylvia's and hit her—opportunity. She hadn't seemed as upset about Sylvia hassling her about her front yard gardens, but perhaps she had been. Motive. With her swinging tools around all day while gardening, she was definitely strong enough. She had the means.

Hmm... had I just discovered the killer?

CHAPTER 7

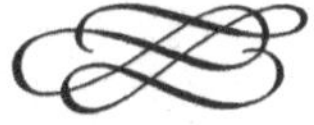

I SPENT most of the night tossing and turning, wondering if Ruby could be right. Had Tina murdered Sylvia? Was her reaction to finding the body simply an act? Had she realized she'd messed up and hadn't wiped down the hammer, then concocted her story of picking it up at the murder scene? I struggled to remember if I'd seen her carry it when she'd crossed the street that morning. Unable to recall, I also speculated she could have hidden it in her sweatshirt or the waistband of her pants. Just because I hadn't noticed it didn't necessarily mean she didn't have it.

In the morning, as I sat at the kitchen island sipping my coffee, a knock sounded at the back door.

"Dang it," I whispered when I saw Darla carrying enough food to feed the seven people who were supposed to be staying at my home.

"Come in, come in," I said, stepping aside as she hurried past me into the kitchen, her blonde ponytail bobbing.

"This cinnamon cake is still hot," she said, setting it down on the counter. "I also made Eggs Benedict, cut up some fruit, and squeezed some fresh orange juice. Jack is bringing that in."

I turned to find Mr. Dimples strolling through the back door. "Hey, Bernie!"

"Hi."

"Everything okay?"

I nodded. The two obviously hadn't seen the news; too busy being lovestruck and staring into at each other's eyes all night.

Well, that's what I figured, anyway.

"Did I hear Jack?" Ruby yelled as she hurried in from the living room. "My stars, I certainly did. Isn't he just as hot as the surface of the sun?" With a gasp, she laid her hand over her heart and batted her eyelashes in his direction.

"What time are your guests coming down?" Darla asked as she pulled out some plates from the cabinet. "Should we set the table now, or are they late risers?"

"There aren't any guests," I said.

Darla and Jack exchanged glances as she set the dishes back on the shelf. "Why didn't you call?" she asked. "To cancel?"

"Were they no-shows?" Jack asked.

"I didn't call because I forgot. The woman across the street was murdered yesterday and things were pretty crazy around here. Phoning you to cancel breakfast completely slipped my mind."

Both stared at me slack-jawed. I had been right. They'd been too busy being lovey-dovey to watch the news.

Jack shook his head and scrubbed his hand over his cheek, as if he could rub away the dimple. "Tell us what happened, Bernie."

I had previously shared my run-ins with Sylvia with both of them, so they weren't surprised by her antics. But the fact the whole neighborhood had an issue with her? That shocked them.

By the time I finished my story of Tina finding the body, the eardrum shattering scream and me running over to the house, they'd each retrieved a cup of coffee and taken a seat at the kitchen island.

"Unbelievable," Darla muttered. "I understand

why you forgot to cancel your order with me."

"I'm so sorry about that," I said. "I'm not sure what to do with all this food. I'll never be able to eat it." Well, based on the tantalizing scent, I could certainly make a large dent in the cinnamon cake with little to no effort.

"No worries," Darla said, pulling out her phone. "I know what to do."

I decided not to question her plan, but roll with it instead.

Ten minutes later, my doorbell rang. "We were summoned," Jezebel said when I answered. "Darla says you've got a bunch of food that needs to be eaten."

I smiled as I took her in an embrace. "I do."

"Good. I brought the walking garbage disposal." She hitched a thumb over her shoulder at her boyfriend, Gunner. "He's a bottomless pit."

The huge man also hugged me, his beard tickling my cheek. "Watch it, woman. You've been known to put away more than your fair share, too."

Based on their ripped physiques, one would never guess such a thing.

"Hey, Jezzy!" Ruby yelled. "Hold still! I'm trying to imagine you with a personality!"

I repeated the insult and Jezebel laughed. The

two had always greeted each other with zingers while alive and had continued when Jezebel discovered Ruby was stuck on this plane.

"Hey, Ruby! Your face makes onions cry!"

After a good chuckle, we filed back into the kitchen. Darla had retrieved the plates once again and scooped out Eggs Benedict, fruit, and cinnamon cake, then poured fresh juice for everyone while I caught up Gunner and Jezebel on the latest neighborhood gossip.

"So now the sheriff thinks I have something do with it," I said, rolling my eyes as we settled in around the dining room table.

"You did say you wanted to kill her," Gunner said. With a wink, he took a big bite of the eggs.

"A figure of speech. I'd never hurt her."

"Oh, come on," Darla teased. "Remember that time on our way back from shopping? Sylvia was out in her front yard? You told me you wanted to run her over."

"But that doesn't mean I'd actually do it," I said. "People say things they don't mean all the time."

"I don't," Ruby said. "When I say Jack looks like a Greek god and I should be his one and only goddess, I mean it." She leaned over and kissed his cheek.

He glanced around the table and narrowed his gaze on me. "She's next to me, isn't she?"

I nodded. "And saying a bunch of stuff I'm not going to repeat."

Just as he was about to protest, Adam's voice sounded from the front door. "Hello?"

After hurrying into the entryway, I hugged him and settled my head against his chest, his unexpected visit both thrilling and surprising me. "What are you doing here?"

"I had to interview Tina. I saw the crew arrive while I was there and thought I'd drop in."

"We're having the breakfast that was supposed to be for my full house today."

"Ah. They canceled, right?"

"No," I replied, stepping away. "They arrived, but then scattered when the sheriff yelled that we were in the middle of a murder investigation."

Adam pursed his lips and winced. "Oh, no. Sorry about that."

"Do you want something to eat?" I asked hopefully, squeezing his hand.

"Sure. I can stay for a bit."

As we entered the dining room, everyone greeted him. I'd become so close to all in the room, I realized being with them was like settling down with family I loved and adored. My heart filled with joy as I stared at my friends.

"We were just talking about the murder across the street," Darla said. "And all the times Bernie threatened to hurt Sylvia, in her offhanded way, of course."

I smiled and took a sip of my juice. "She was the one who threatened me," I replied. "She wanted to take away my livelihood, so you're correct, I didn't have anything good to say about her."

Jezebel shook her head. "She can't do that now, right? You and your neighbors can go about your business."

Glancing over at Adam, I noted he'd quit eating and stared at me. I dabbed my mouth with my napkin and smiled.

"At least you're dating a cop," Darla said, then pointed her fork at Adam and grinned. "You'll need to inform the sheriff that he needs to back off on pursuing Bernie as a suspect."

She had been teasing, but Adam shook his head, his gaze serious. "I can't do that."

Darla set down her fork, her brow furrowed. "Why not?"

"Because it's an active investigation," Adam said, shrugging. "Everyone has to be considered a suspect until they've been cleared. That's the way these things work."

An uncomfortable silence settled over the table. Everyone except Jack had quit eating, their gazes jumping from me to Adam.

"I don't understand," Darla said. "Bernie's your girlfriend, right?"

Adam nodded.

"Do you honestly think in your heart of hearts that you're dating a murderer?"

"No, I don't."

"Then what's the issue?" Darla asked.

Adam cleared his throat and set down his napkin as if trying to gather his thoughts. After a moment, he smiled. "The issue is that a woman is dead. There are steps to an investigation that must be taken. Unfortunately, Bernie has found herself in the middle of it. She has said some things she probably shouldn't have. She found the body. She'll be carefully scrutinized, just like everyone else involved. When our office feels that she's in the clear and had nothing to do with Sylvia's death, then we won't investigate her any further."

"That's ridiculous," Darla said, rolling her eyes.

I wiggled in my chair, the tension in the room gripping me like a vise.

"It is, but that's the way these things go," Jezebel said. She also knew the ins and outs of an investigation because Gunner was in law enforcement as well.

"Wait a minute," Gunner said. "There's nothing ridiculous about doing a deep dive into someone who had threatened to kill the murder victim in the past... even if she is dating a cop."

"Thank you," Adam muttered.

"She's your *girlfriend*," Darla said. "You're supposed to love and trust her. Investigating her for a murder you know she didn't commit not only seems like a waste of the sheriff's department resources, but if I was Bernie, I'd also question my relationship with you. Do I really want to date someone who thinks I'm capable of murder?"

Darla was on a roll. With each passing moment, she became more irritated. Her cheeks flamed red, and I swore her irises had dilated.

"It's fine," I said, shooting Jack a glare. Why didn't he try to calm her down? Did she truly feel this way or was this her schizophrenia?

"How can you say that it's fine for your boyfriend to think you're a killer?" Darla shouted, shooting to her feet.

"I agree," Jack said, also standing. "I think it's pretty awful of you, Adam."

"I'm just doing my job," he said through a clenched jaw.

"Look, it's not a big deal," I said. "The sheriff's department won't find anything because I've done nothing but run my mouth when I shouldn't have."

Darla shook her head. "You're being foolish, Bernie. And Adam should be standing up for you. I'll see you all later."

As she and Jack headed for the kitchen, I stared at the table and wondered how things had spun out of control so quickly. One moment I had the warm and fuzzies settling in my chest from being with my friends that I considered family, the next, a cold stone of fear had taken its place.

I expected the police to interview me and quickly dismiss me as a suspect. I thought I was no longer on their radar. But apparently, I still sat in the crosshairs, a potential murder charge hanging over my head.

"We better head out as well," Jezebel said. "I've got inventory at the bar."

"Thanks for coming over and helping us with the food," I said, trying to remain upbeat.

Gunner gave me a hug. "If you didn't off your neighbor, you've got nothing to worry about."

Tell that to all the people in prison for crimes they didn't commit.

After they left, Adam gathered all the plates. We stood at the sink, both of our hands covered in warm, soapy water, and washed dishes. A simple act, one that I loved doing with my boyfriend. Frankly, I wouldn't mind washing dishes with him for the rest of my life.

If I wasn't put away for murder, which wasn't going to happen if I had anything to say about it. I couldn't shake the sinking feeling in the pit of my stomach, the one that told me I couldn't sit around and wait for something to happen. I needed to help myself.

"Adam, if I'm still a suspect like you indicated at breakfast, I feel like I should do something."

He handed me a dish to dry. "Like what?"

I quickly wiped down my soapy hands, then took the plate and did the same. "Maybe just snoop around and talk to some of my neighbors."

"The police are talking to your neighbors."

"I know, but people seem to share more with me than they do with anyone in your department."

He sighed, his shoulders sagging. Suddenly, he

looked much older than his thirty-six years. Was it the job, or was it me?

Laying my wet hand on his wrist, I said, "You can't expect me to sit around and do nothing."

"Bernie, I—"

"I'll tell you everything I find out," I said. "Everything. We worked so well together last time. Remember? We were a team. We can do that again."

After turning off the water, he faced me and sighed. For a long moment, he simply stared at me and I thought he may arrest me just to keep me off the case. Finally, he said, "If we're going to do this, you need to be careful."

"Of course," I said, smiling. "I'm always careful."

"Woohoo!" Ruby yelled from the dining room. "It's about dang time! Let's go solve a murder!"

CHAPTER 8

THE NEXT DAY, only one person remained out in front of my house. Apparently, the murder had lived its life through the news cycle. The woman stood on my driveway, staring at Sylvia's house. Black jeans hugged her thin legs, and I noted she was also a fan of black hoodies. Yellow crime scene tape still crossed Sylvia's driveway, but the police had closed the garage door.

Who was the woman? I recognized her from the prior day. Why was she so intent on being at the scene of the murder?

"Do you think she's related to Sylvia?" I asked Ruby as we both stared out the window.

"If she was, why would she stand there staring at the house?"

Valid point. "Maybe she's scoping out the house and is going to rob it?"

"She's not very sneaky," Ruby said, shaking her head. "I would think if she were planning to burgle it, she'd be hiding and not calling attention to herself. She doesn't care who sees her."

What else could she be doing? "Do you think she's one of those people obsessed with death and murder scenes?"

Ruby shrugged. "Why don't you just go ask? If she is, maybe she can offer you some insight into murder junkies and whether you should advertise to them."

I hated speaking to strangers, but Ruby had a point. Desperate times called for desperate measures. I needed to move out of my comfort zone.

After pasting a smile on my face, I opened the front door and strode down the walkway. A police car sat in front of Wilder's house—they were most likely getting his statement. The woman turned. In her twenties, black hair framed her pale face while black eyeliner circled her blue eyes. She stared at me expectantly, but without a smile.

"Hi," I said, giving her a little wave. "Were you related to Sylvia?"

She gazed back at the house and shook her head. "I'm… I'm fascinated with life after death. What's there, if anything? Having been murdered and her life taken so quickly, could she be trapped on Earth with us?"

I glanced over at Ruby, who shrugged. "I haven't seen anything indicating old Slimy Sylvia is still with us in spirit, but you're the ghost whisperer, not me."

"Have you been out here all night?" I asked the stranger.

"No. I tried to sleep here, but the cops came by and told me to come back at daylight. I thought you were the one who had called them since I'm out in front of your house."

"It wasn't me," I said, glancing at the murder scene. "So, you think you may be able to see the dead woman's ghost?"

The woman nodded. "I'm hoping to. I'd love to be able to interact with her, to ask her questions."

Wait a minute. Had I just found another person who could speak with the dead? I didn't know whether to be frightened or excited.

After clearing my throat, I asked, "Like what? The things you mentioned before?"

"Yes. And to see if she knows who killed her. I'd love to be able to solve the case."

Wouldn't we all. "So, have you spoken to dead people before?" I asked.

She shook her head. "I feel an energy with the other side. Like they're trying to communicate with me, but they can't quite get through. I'm attempting to open myself up to them so they can speak with me."

Ruby moved directly in front of her, their noses about a half inch apart. "I'm right here, sweetheart. You can't see me. You can't hear me. Sorry, but I think you're full of the brown stuff."

"What's your name?" I asked. "Where are you from?"

The woman turned to me and smiled. "Luna. Luna Howler. I live in Phoenix."

Strange name. "It's nice to meet you. I'm Bernie. I own the bed and breakfast."

Her eyes widened as she turned to look at my house. "That's a bed and breakfast?"

"Yes."

"Do you have any rooms available?"

I almost lied and said no. Did I really want Luna Howler, the person trying to connect with the dead woman across the street, staying with me? But then I realized the absurdity of my hesitation. I was the woman who spoke to my dead grandmother many times throughout the day.

"Sure," I replied, hoping I didn't regret my decision. We discussed the room rate, and she didn't blink when I gave her my price.

"That's wonderful," she replied. "Do you have a room that overlooks the house across the street?"

"I don't." Hopefully that wouldn't be a deal breaker. "But the living room is comfortable, and you have a bird's-eye view of the house. Also, the police won't be coming by and telling you to move on."

She glanced from my house back to Sylvia's and grinned. "It sounds perfect. Let me grab my bag. I slept in my car last night parked down the street, so I'd love a shower."

I smiled, thrilled I had a bit of money coming in. "Well, now that you're a guest, why don't you park in my back lot?"

"This is wonderful. I feel like the universe has connected us for a reason. I'm so pleased!"

As Luna trotted down the street to fetch her vehicle, Ruby asked, "Why do you think she drove two hours to a murder scene? Doesn't Phoenix have its own people killing each other?"

"Great question," I muttered as Luna pulled

around the back of the house and Ruby and I followed. "I'll definitely ask."

Once she'd parked and hauled her duffel bag out of the trunk, I led her in through the back door. Usually, guests always came in through the front, but it seemed ridiculous to make her walk all the way around just so she could be wowed by my grand living room.

As we rounded the corner from the kitchen to the dining room, she gasped as we entered said room.

"This is magnificent," she whispered, taking in the high ceilings, the sweeping staircase, and the large brick fireplace.

"Thanks. My grandmother built it and left it to me when she died."

"The universe has blessed you."

Ruby snorted and rolled her eyes. "Didn't she just hear you? *I* blessed you. *Not* the dang universe."

"Luna, what brought you to Sedona?" I asked. "Was it Sylvia's murder, or something else?"

"I was here for a spiritual retreat when I heard of her untimely demise. I thought I'd check it out and see if I could contact her."

Even though I was the one who could speak to ghosts, Luna made me slightly uncomfortable, but I wasn't sure why. "Let's get you checked in and I'll show you to your room." With a smile, I waved for her to follow me to the small check-in desk tucked away in the corner.

After she filled out the information on the iPad, I held my breath as I ran her credit card and sighed with relief when it went through. Money in my account gave me the warm and fuzzies. "Let's go upstairs and get you that shower," I said.

"Wonderful," Luna replied, trailing behind me. "I simply can't believe my good fortune of your house being a bed and breakfast. Me finding you was meant to be."

When I stopped at the top of the stairs, Ruby yelled, "Duh, duh, duh! The Death Room!"

After opening the door to the room on the right where the drug trafficker had met his demise, I smiled as Luna stepped in. If she wanted to communicate with the dead, it was probably the best place for her.

"Thank you," she said, glancing around the space. "This is perfect. I'm so thrilled our paths have crossed."

"Would you like some coffee? Tea?"

She turned to me and grinned. "A shower first, then some coffee would be wonderful."

I shut the door and hurried down to the

kitchen to fire up the coffee maker. When a knock sounded at the front door, I went to answer it. To my utter shock, Wilder, my neighbor, stood on my doorstep, his face paler than usual. His perfectly combed beard seemed a little messy and I realized he was upset.

"What's going on?" I asked.

"May I come in?"

"Of course."

No smile. Definitely had some things on his mind.

Once we were settled on the couches, he rubbed his hands together and stared at me. "I was wondering what you told the police about the morning Sylvia was murdered."

I arched an eyebrow and pursed my lips together as I gathered my thoughts. "Well, I went out to plant my petunias, then I saw Tina head over to Sylvia's house. A while later she screamed, and I ran over there. Why?"

"Someone told them they saw me walking this way that morning."

"What does that have to do with anything?"

"The police think that because this house is at the dead end of the cul-de-sac and across from Sylvia's, I have no business walking this way."

They had a point. Unless he walked out into the desert—or into Sylvia's garage to kill her—he really didn't have any reason to be down at this end of the street.

"Were you walking this way that morning?" I asked.

He nodded. "I have a place out in the desert where I enjoy meditation as the sun rises."

"What time?" Even though I had nothing to do with the information that had been handed over to the police, I was curious about Wilder's movements before sunrise.

"About five-thirty."

"I didn't call anything in," I said, laughing. "Trust me, I wasn't even conscious at that time of the day."

He sighed and rubbed his face. "Sylvia had called the city about the herb store I run out of the house. I'd received a notice from them instructing me to get the proper permits. I hate dealing with the city and state taxes, permits, etcetera. I just want to be left in peace."

I sympathized with him. "I understand. I've got a tax bill hanging over my head that I need to deal with, but I keep putting it off."

"The police say they'll be in touch," Wilder

continued. "I'm not to leave town because I'm a suspect."

"I assume everyone on the street will be questioned. We all tangled with her in one way or the other."

"So they've interviewed you as well?"

I nodded and sat back against the cushions. "Yes. Even though I'm dating a cop I'm still on the list."

Wilder shook his head, then stood. "I better get going. I also want to talk to Pete, Yolanda, and Tina. Someone told the cops they saw me that morning and I'd like to know why. I've been kind to everyone and I keep to myself. My yard is tidy. Why would someone turn me in like this? I feel like I'm being stabbed in the back… set up, somehow, by someone on this street."

"I don't know who would have done such a thing, Wilder. I can only assure you it wasn't me."

Not that I'd tell him if I had. I hated confrontation.

After we said our goodbyes, I returned to the kitchen to check the coffee pot. The brewing cycle had concluded, and the hot liquid was ready for my guest.

"You know, if Wilder didn't do anything, he

shouldn't be so worried about the cops," Ruby said when she appeared next to me.

"I didn't do anything, and I'm concerned," I whispered.

"Remember when we saw the body?" Ruby asked. "Did it strike you as fairly fresh?"

Despite her vulgarity, I thought back to Tina hovering over Sylvia. She'd been the one to check for a pulse. I didn't recall her saying anything about Sylvia's skin temperature, but I did remember the blood wasn't congealed.

"We need to find out the time of death," Ruby continued. "If she died a couple of hours before we found her, Wilder could have gone for his early morning walk, noticed Sylvia leaving for work, picked up Tina's hammer, and pummeled her in a fit of rage."

"Because she turned him in to the city for running an illegal business out of his house?" I whispered.

"Exactly."

Ruby's theory made perfect sense and it was definitely something to consider. Wilder had always struck me as a little strange, but never violent. During the neighborhood meeting, he'd made it clear he didn't like confrontation. But maybe in a state of anger, he lost his calm mojo and swung a hammer at Sylvia.

Perhaps Wilder wasn't the zen-like master of emotions I had originally suspected. If that were the case, I'd have to make sure I wasn't alone with him and if I did find myself in such a precarious position, I'd carefully choose my words.

I didn't want a hammer crashing my skull.

CHAPTER 9

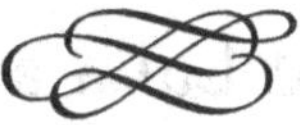

WITH MY PAYING customer snuggled up on my couch watching the murder scene across the street while sipping her coffee, I sneaked out the back door. Was she one of those people who drank the magical caffeinated elixir all day and slept without issue, or was she planning on staring at Sylvia's house all night long?

I didn't have time to hang out and discover her motives. Clearing my name was at the top of my important things to do list, so I headed across the street to Yolanda's. Did I think she killed Sylvia? No. But she did speak to everyone on the block and liked to talk. Maybe she'd spill some information I could pass on to Adam.

Despite my attempts to convince Ruby to stay

at the house and watch our guest, she insisted on coming with me. I'd assumed she'd be interested in trying to connect with the woman who wanted to talk to the dead, but she was focused on seeing my neighbor.

"Can't wait to see LaLa and watch you try to talk your way out of her dirt-tasting tea!"

"A simple no is all it takes," I muttered as we approached her front door.

"That was the first time. She's going to be strong-arming you. Trust me."

With a sigh, I plastered a smile on my face and knocked. I heard footsteps inside and the door opened a crack, revealing my neighbor's face. Her brow furrowed. "I wish you would've called, Bernie."

"Sorry. I just wanted to talk to you for a few minutes." Why didn't she let me in?

"Let me get my robe on," she sighed. "Hold on."

"She's running around with her pert little butt hanging out," Ruby said. "As a general rule, she hates clothes."

Frankly, I could understand her stance fairly easily. Bras? They were the worst. Too tight jeans? Couldn't wait to slip them off at the end of the day. Heavy coats, shoes that didn't fit right, underwear that shrank in the wash... it was all uncomfortable. But that didn't mean I had any desire to run around my house—or my yard—naked. Just the thought made my skin crawl. But what did that say about me? Maybe my body issues were deeper than I understood. More self-discovery to push to the back burner and not think about.

A few moments passed before the door opened again. Yolanda stood before me in a golden robe covering her from her neck to her ankles, reminding me of some ethereal deity who didn't belong on this plane. A goddess.

"Come on in," she said, stepping aside and gesturing for me to enter. "Would you like some tea?"

"Told you," Ruby muttered. "It's always about the dang tea. I loved this woman while alive, but the tea always grated on my nerves."

"No, thank you," I said, taking the same seat on the couch I had during our neighborhood meeting.

"Are you sure? It's really good for you. I'm brewing one for a gentle detox filled with antioxidants."

"I'm fine, thank you."

She shook her head. "Suit yourself. I could

never get your grandmother to drink it, either. Sometimes when she finally did accept a cup, I could've sworn she dumped it in my plants." Busted. I glanced over at Ruby, who simply shrugged. "Let me grab my mug and I'll be right back."

When she returned and folded herself into the cushions on the opposite end of the couch with her tea, which did indeed smell like moldy dirt, she smiled. "What can I do for you?"

I realized I really didn't have any specific questions for Yolanda, and I was on a fishing expedition. "I was wondering if the police had been here and what you told them."

"The sheriff was here for a little while yesterday, but he needed to leave. Apparently, my plants caused him allergy issues. His eyes swelled and he began having coughing fits. He said he'd send someone by in the next day or two."

"Sounds like Bruce," Ruby muttered. "Horrible allergies."

"I saw the cops at Wilder's home earlier," I said. "Then he came to see me. Has he been here?"

She shook her head. "No. But I've been gone most of the day. What did he have to say to you?"

I sighed and ran my hand over the blue cushion. "He wasn't happy the police were at his home. Someone reported he was walking down the street toward Sylvia's house the morning she was murdered. He thought it may have been me."

Yolanda arched an eyebrow. "Did you?"

"No. He apparently goes out into the desert to watch the sun rise and meditate. I promise you, I'm not up at the crack of dawn."

"Hmm... were you aware of the habit of his?"

"Not until he told me. As you know, he was very upset Sylvia turned him into the city for running a business out of his house."

"Oh, yes. He's upset," she said. "The more he's off the grid, the happier he is. Did you know he doesn't own a TV or a radio?"

"No. What about a computer?"

She shook her head. "He's got his phone, but that's it. He's right out of the stone age."

I'd considered unplugging before and living my life without the constant chatter of society. No internet, no television, no radio. Just me, my thoughts, and my talkative ghost. However, I relied on the internet to run my business... everything from advertising to ordering supplies to taking reservations. Even if I wanted to go off the grid, I didn't think it would be feasible.

"Interesting..." Yolanda tapped the side of her mug with her short, manicured nail.

"What?"

"I was just thinking... what if Wilder killed Sylvia?"

"Great minds think alike," Ruby said. "She's got the same ideas as you and me."

"I mean, everyone has a hammer lying around," Yolanda continued. "And if he was angry enough at her reporting his illegal business to the city... there's his motive."

She didn't realize the hammer belonged to Tina and had been left in her front yard overnight, so I filled her in. "What he could've done is gone for his morning walk, noticed Sylvia in the garage, and grabbed Tina's hammer in a fit of rage," I concluded.

Her eyes widened as she set down her tea on the coffee table. "Oh, my goodness. Have you told the police about this?"

When I'd spoken to Adam earlier, he'd said we wouldn't be seeing each other for the rest of the day. "Not yet. I'm meeting with Adam tomorrow and thought I'd share it with him then." The theory didn't sit well with me. The pacifist who just wanted to be left alone losing his cool and killing his neighbor? Based on what I'd seen from Pete, it seemed more his style, not Wilder's.

"Well, I really hate to say this, but it's sure

been peaceful around here not knowing if Sylvia's spying on me or not," Yolanda said. "I spent a few hours out in my backyard working on the rose bushes and meditating before running my errands. No one looking over the fence, no one yelling at me to put clothes on. I feel as though I've got my life back."

It was hard to hear a woman claim she'd rather walk around naked than have her neighbor breathing, but I understood to a certain extent. Yolanda had lived in her home a long time and had done what she pleased until Sylvia moved in. Heck, she'd even semi-joked about buying the woman out of her home.

I still hadn't recovered from the shock of finding Sylvia, having thousands of dollars slip through my fingers, my friends fighting, being a murder suspect, the press camped in front of my house and my new, strange visitor, who I appreciated very much. There hadn't been a lot of time to consider my life without Sylvia because even in death, she'd been a thorn in my side. It all stemmed from her.

"Hopefully, things will get back to normal for me sooner rather than later," I said.

"It's definitely been a relief," Yolanda replied, sighing.

It occurred to me she didn't seem too upset her next-door neighbor had been killed. In fact, it had been somewhat of a blessing for her. Not the rest of us on the street, though. Pete had told Sylvia to drop dead. She'd been killed with Tina's hammer. Her threats of closing down my business had been real, and unless Wilder got his permits in order, the same would happen for him, as well.

Yolanda was the only one coming out unscathed.

"You know, I loved hanging out with your grandmother," she said. "She was crazy fun, and she loved you to bits."

I smiled and glanced at my ghost.

"She shared with me the heartache she went through when she was young and her parents took away her daughter," Yolanda continued. "How she tried so hard to have a relationship and how difficult it had been. When your mother had you and you were old enough to come visit, her main focus was building a relationship with you. She always told me she knew you were special."

My cheeks burned at the compliment. "I loved her very much."

"The feeling was mutual, Bernie. You were

lucky to have such an amazing woman in your life."

"I agree." Glancing out the window, I noted darkness had fallen and thought I had better touch bases with Luna to see if she'd detected Sylvia's spirit walking around. If yes, I wanted to be certain I went the other way. "I better get home. I've got one guest I need to check in on."

"Sure," Yolanda said. "Do you think the murderer is someone on this street, or do you think it someone from the outside?"

"I don't know," I replied, walking to the door. "All I'm certain of is that I didn't do it."

"Yes. It does give me a little bit of the willies thinking one of our neighbors could've killed her though."

I smiled, but my gut churned with discontent. "Agreed."

As I strode across the street, I tried to dismiss the fact that Yolanda was the only one to come out unscathed. What if she'd killed Sylvia and was perfectly content to let one of her neighbors take the fall?

She knew Sylvia's routine since they'd lived next door to each other. She had a bird's-eye view of Tina's house and would have noticed the hammer lying in the front yard. And the motive...

well, she now had her privacy back. "Motive, opportunity, and means," I muttered.

"What?" Ruby asked.

"Nothing," I whispered as I unlocked the back door. After walking into the kitchen and flipping on the lights, I noted the dining room was dark, as was the living room.

"Luna?" I called as I turned on the dining room switch.

"Shh," she whispered. "Don't turn on any more lights!"

I squinted into the living room to find her, Ruby's ghostly form a few steps ahead of me.

"The crazy turnip is over by the windows," she said. "Follow me."

I found my guest kneeling on the floor staring out into the night. "What are you doing?" I asked, slowly lowering myself down next to her.

"Do you see her?"

"See what?" Ruby asked.

I had no idea. "Um... no?"

"Be still and quiet," Luna whispered as she held up her phone. I glanced at the screen and realized she was filming Sylvia's house.

Across the street, the living room curtains had been left open. I could make out the outline of a couch. Maybe a fake tree? I didn't see anything overly suspicious.

"There it is," Luna whispered. I gasped as I stared at the phone. A small, white light seemed to be moving in the back of the house, barely visible to me. "It's her soul. It's like she's a firefly."

I glanced up at Ruby who shook her head. "That's no one's soul. That's someone robbing that house."

"Let's go over," Luna whispered as she stood upright. "Let's talk to her and find out who killed her."

I agreed, but like Ruby, I didn't think Sylvia would be on this plane as something resembling a firefly. Maybe a hornet or black beetle.

"T-That's not a good idea," I stammered, feeling my pockets for my phone. Where had I left the darn thing?

Luna ignored me and opened the front door, then raced across the street.

"Oh, heck. You better go after her," Ruby said. "She's going to get her brains knocked in just like Sylvia."

My heart thundered as Ruby and I followed Luna.

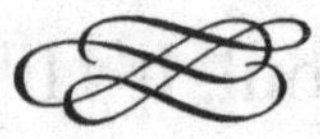

CHAPTER 10

THE FRONT DOOR WAS LOCKED, so we crept around the back. Sweat dotted my brow despite the cool night air while nerves twisted my belly. I should've called the police instead of agreeing to follow Luna.

"Hasn't Adam told you there's a fine line between stupidity and bravery?" Ruby asked as she tiptoed next to me. I nodded.

"I think you've crossed it. This is dumb, even by my standards, Bernie."

Duly noted.

The sliding glass door leading out to the back-yard stood wide open. Luna stared at it a moment, her brow furrowed in confusion. "Maybe she likes fresh air," she muttered. Or maybe the intruder did, but I didn't bother to mention the possibility.

I stepped over the threshold and held my breath as I listened. Someone was in the back bedrooms... opening and closing drawers. At my feet lay a white PVC pipe about the same length as the track of the sliding glass door. Sylvia had probably used it as a security measure to lock the door. Either she hadn't set it in the morning she'd been killed, or I had been wrong about an intruder and the ghost could move inanimate objects *and* enjoyed fresh air.

Gripping the pipe, I carried it over my shoulder like a baseball bat as I slowly strode toward the hallway. The further we went inside the house, the staler the air became, even though the home had only been empty a couple of days. *Death. This is the remnants of death.* Again, I thought about leaving and calling the police, but what if it was the murderer? What if I could solve the case right then and get back to my life? If I abandoned the confrontation, the killer may slip away, never to be seen again.

"Sylvia?" Luna called. I gasped and stilled. What the heck was she thinking? "Are you here?"

"Sylvia's not here, you idiot!" Ruby yelled. "But

now you've let whoever is back there know you are!"

"We come in peace," Luna continued. "We're here to help you."

Long moments passed as silence blanketed the house. Whoever was in back had gone quiet.

Ruby was right. This was dumb. I shouldn't be in this house confronting a potential killer with a PVC pipe and a woman who hunted for firefly spirits.

"I'm coming out," a deep voice said from the back of the house. "I'm unarmed."

"That doesn't sound like a woman," Luna said. "Do spirits' voice change once they're released from their bodies?"

Ignoring her, I kept my gaze firmly on the hallway, still gripping my pipe with sweaty hands. Ruby ran in front of me as far as possible, but fell just short of being able to glance down the dark corridor. She motioned me to move closer. I, however, wanted as much space between me and the intruder as possible so I could assess the situation: run like heck, or swing at him?

The hallway light went on, and I blinked a few times to allow my eyes to adjust. A man standing about six foot and weighing two hundred pounds walked slowly toward us, his hands raised to his shoulders. Brown hair, but I couldn't make out any distinct facial features.

"That's not a spirit," Luna said, placing her hands on her hips. "What the heck is going on here?"

"I'm sorry?" the man said.

"Stop right there," I told him, pointing the pipe at him as he entered the living room. "Who are you and what are you doing in Sylvia's house?"

"Bernie, I've got to say, you're looking pretty dang fierce standing there like that," Ruby said. "Like you're ready to hunt zombies in the great apocalypse. I'm impressed."

I must appear much braver than I felt. My insides had turned to goo and my knees shook, but if I resembled someone who regularly kicked some butt and took names, I'd keep up the charade. "Answer me!" I yelled, smacking the wall with my pipe. "Who are you?"

Ruby let out a low whistle. Luna yelped and covered her ears with her hands, then whispered, "I hate violence."

Many different ideas went through my mind: another spirit hunter or a robber being my top two guesses. I wasn't prepared for the real answer.

"My name's Cody," the man said. "I'm Sylvia's ex-husband."

Ah, the cheater who left her for another woman. Sylvia had shared she'd been thrilled to toss him out of her life.

"What are you doing here?" I asked.

He sighed and lowered his hands to his sides. "I... I'm not sure... I can't believe someone killed her. I had to come." As he stared at me, tears pooled in his eyes and his shoulders sagged. A man defeated. Or a man giving an Oscar worthy performance. "Can I ask who you are?"

For being a no-good cheater, he sure seemed upset. Slowly, I lowered my pipe, but kept gripping the end, just in case. "My name's Bernie. I live across the street and saw your flashlight."

It was then I realized Luna was still muttering about Sylvia being a firefly. "Why don't you go back to the house?" I said, turning to her. "I'll be fine."

She glanced at Cody, shook her head as if profoundly unable to believe she hadn't encountered a spirit camouflaged as a firefly, then nodded and retreated out the back door.

"They said one of the neighbors found her," Cody said. "Was that you?"

"Sort of. Why are you sneaking around in her house after dark?"

"Can we sit down?" Cody asked.

"I think it's best if we head outside," I said. "It's my understanding this is still an active crime scene."

"But she died in the garage?"

"I'm not a cop but I'm sure neither of us are supposed to be in here." In fact, I could practically hear Adam lecturing me about it.

We stepped out the back door and he slid it shut. "I thought I'd have to break in, but this wasn't locked."

Interesting. Another little detail I'd have to share with Adam.

In the moonlight, I made out his facial features. Square jaw, a small scar below his left eye, and a goatee. Probably in his late thirties, early forties.

A chill traveled over me. I wished I'd grabbed my sweater before heading out on this adventure.

"I'm still confused on why you're here," I said. "Sylvia made it very clear there wasn't any love lost between the two of you. If I remember correctly, you have a kid with a woman in Cottonwood."

He rubbed his face and suddenly aged ten years. I seemed to have that effect on men—first Adam, and now Cody. All within a span of a couple of days. Probably not a good thing. "It was a mistake. One night of sex that ruined my life. I loved Sylvia with my whole heart. When she found out about the baby, she left me. I've tried to do the right thing... I pay child support, but the mother doesn't want me in her life. She just wants my monthly check."

Hmm... a very different story than his ex-wife had shared.

"The scent of liar is pretty strong in here," Ruby said, standing on her tiptoes in front of Cody, almost nose-to-nose.

"I smell lavender," he said, glancing around the yard. "Sylvia hated lavender, but she must have a plant around here somewhere."

Nope. Just my grandmother's ghost.

"Anyway, when the police came and told me she'd been killed... I..." Tears welled in his eyes again. "It felt like my life was ending. I always thought we'd have time to... to be together again, but now, we don't."

I lightly tapped the pipe against my shin, almost feeling sorry for the man. He seemed quite distraught. "But why are you *here*?"

"To be close to all that's left of her," he whispered. "To smell her favorite perfume. To touch her pillow again. To... to try to be as near to her as I can for just a little while longer."

As the tears fell, I realized Cody wasn't the monster Sylvia had made him out to be. Maybe she'd been the liar, which wouldn't be that far of a stretch. I'd caught her being less than truthful to the police when she called in the epic party I'd supposedly thrown.

"We... we weren't good to each other," he continued. "She had an affair as well. I don't know with who, but she admitted it to me. I had hoped we'd start over, but then she left me. I always thought I'd be able to eventually get her back. That we'd work things out."

It certainly wasn't my place to point out that Pete, who lived down the street, had had an affair with Sylvia. Maybe she'd had more than one. I didn't want to break Cody's heart any more than it had been. The last bit of my armor faded, and pity overcame me. "I'm sorry for your loss," I said.

"Thanks." He wiped his face with the back of his hand. "I know I shouldn't be here, and I apologize if I scared you. I just feel so... lost."

No firefly spirits, no burglars... just a sad man looking to connect with the dead woman he'd loved. I wanted to cry right along with him.

"I'll leave you to it," I said.

"Please don't tell the cops I'm here," he begged. "I don't want any trouble."

Unsure if I could honor my word, I simply nodded and crossed my fingers behind my back. "Take care."

With a sigh, I walked around the house and out the side yard. It wasn't until I crossed the street that I realized I still held the PVC pipe.

"Why didn't you tell me to drop this?" I hissed at Ruby as we approached the back door. "I shouldn't be carrying it!"

"I didn't notice," she said. "Don't blame me for you taking evidence from a crime scene." She floated through the back door, leaving me staring at the pipe.

She was right. I had removed evidence. Crud. For a second, I thought about turning around and setting it back at Sylvia's where I'd found it, but I didn't want to have another meeting with Cody. I tossed it in the dirt and entered my house, suddenly exhausted.

I paced through the rooms looking for my guest. When I noted her bedroom door closed with the light shining through the crack underneath, I assumed she'd retired for the night, and it was time for me to do the same.

After shutting the door to my own room, I leaned my head against the panel and sighed. Poor Cody. His deep grief pierced my heart. And it also served as a reminder that each day wasn't guaranteed. He'd thought he'd have time to win back Sylvia, but her life had been cut short. Admittedly, they'd both been cruel to their marriage, but the fact he pined for her so deeply moved me.

He obviously loved her. If that was the case, why had he cheated to begin with? Why had she? What had been missing in the relationship that had caused them to turn to others? Did they know? Had they tried to fix it before everything became so broken?

With a sigh, I crawled into bed, focusing on sleep instead of playing marriage counselor.

I smelled her before a cold chill ran over my arm as she lay down with me.

"Where have you been?" I asked, my voice heavy with the sleep just out of reach.

"Haunting the firefly hunter upstairs."

I smiled. "How did that go?"

Ruby chuckled. "I'm a terrible ghost. The one person who is looking for the dead can't even see me."

I opened my eyes and turned on my side to face her. "I'm glad I get to see you."

"Me, too, Bernie," she said. "I think you better have a long talk with Adam tomorrow."

"About what?"

"See if they have an alibi for Cody. I don't believe a word he says."

CHAPTER 11

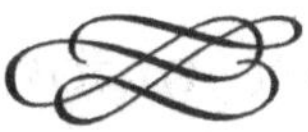

THE NEXT AFTERNOON I headed over to Adam's to compare notes. Would a phone call have been easier? Probably, but now that I had another person under my roof—one who held an intense interest in the murder—I didn't feel comfortable discussing it on the phone while in my house. And I certainly wasn't going to set up shop at Darling's Diner or Canyon Coffee and discuss a killing. Besides, I would get to snuggle Adam while we talked, and if there was one thing I loved to do, it was snuggling my boyfriend.

Of course, Ruby had insisted on going with me, and I couldn't fight her for the exact same reason I couldn't discuss the murder on the phone: my guest. Even though Ned, Adam's ghost, had been clear he would prefer me to leave Ruby at home, I'd have to disappoint him. Trying to appease him and Ruby—she wanted to spend time with him, and he wanted to be left alone—had become an almost impossible task.

As we pulled up in front of Adam's condo, my heart sank when I didn't spot a police vehicle. "He said he'd be back by now," I muttered as I parked.

"The copper's running late," Ruby said. "We'll sit tight and wait for him. Probably got hung up listening to old Bruce-y Boy talk his ear off."

I cut the ignition and leaned my head back against the headrest, still tired despite a good night's rest. A murder and subsequent investigation had that effect on me. Yet, I couldn't wait to hear what the police had uncovered while speaking with Wilder earlier and I wanted to share all the information I'd gathered about Yolanda, Tina, and Cody.

"You know, this investigation stuff suits you," Ruby said. "People dying sucks, but when they do, something inside you comes alive."

Crinkling my nose, I turned to my ghost. "I'm not sure whether to be offended or say thank you."

She shrugged. "Either way is fine with me. I've never cared about offending anyone, and you shouldn't either. I mean, if you're acting like an outright jerk, that's one thing. But if you're going about your life, being kind, and you burrow under someone's skin, the heck with them. You're never going to please everyone. Remember that."

Sage words of wisdom I wished I could follow. Sometimes, my anxiety made it impossible to not care what others thought.

"There he is!" Ruby yelled. "Woohoo! Let's go inside!"

Adam parked as we stepped out of my SUV. He waved and smiled while I hurried over to greet him.

"How's my favorite girlfriend?" he asked as he wrapped his arm around my shoulder and gave me a kiss on my forehead.

"I better be your only girlfriend," I replied. With a snicker, I gently slapped his stomach.

He chuckled and gave me a squeeze. "Of course you are, silly woman. Is Ruby here with you?"

I nodded and we exchanged glances. I'd informed him in the past Ned had asked for me to leave her at home.

"Hi, Ruby," Adam said. "I'm glad you could come over today."

"Me, too, copper. I bet that old coot has missed me." As soon as we were close enough, Ruby ghosted through Adam's condo door. "Ned! Hey, Ned! Where are you?"

"He's not going to be happy," I whispered. "But she insisted."

"We'll have to see what happens," Adam muttered as he slid the key into the lock. "Hopefully there won't be any fighting so we can talk without interruption."

Ruby continued to yell for Ned to show himself.

"She's being relentless," I whispered as Adam set down his keys next to the camera that had caught me breaking into his apartment a few months back. With a shudder, I stared at it. How in the world had I missed the small, round eye staring at me then? Adam had installed it because Ned had been hiding his stuff. Instead, he'd found me breaking his trust.

What a horrible time.

"I'm going to lock up my gun," Adam said. "Help yourself to anything in the kitchen and I'll be back in a flash."

A headache began to form behind my eyes as Ruby sang, "Ned! Come out, come out, wherever you are!" I grabbed a bottle of water and sat down on the couch. "What's wrong with you, old timer! Show yourself!"

I wished she could move more than fifteen feet away from me when out of the house. At least then she could head down the hall and scream for him there instead of in the same room as me.

When Adam returned, he sat next to me and opened his laptop.

"Tell me how things went with the Wilder interview," I said.

He shook his head. "Wilder's a different guy."

I nodded in agreement. "He came by my house after you spoke with him. He was upset and said that someone had called the police on him for walking out into the desert that morning."

"There was more than one call about his early walks," Adam said. "And they all came from Sylvia. She'd called four times before that morning."

"What did the police do?"

"Nothing," he replied with a shrug. "We can't arrest someone for walking down their own street. She claimed she was afraid, and she wanted to file a report so we'd have it if anything were to happen to her. We questioned whether Wilder had ever been violent before but she denied that."

"That's interesting," I said. "'In case something were to happen to her?' Well, something did."

"Yes. Once we put the pieces together, Wilder moved up to our number one suspect on the list."

Ruby turned to me. "Ask him if you're still on the whodunit list. Then ask him where his stupid ghost is."

I sighed and smiled. "Ruby asked if the sheriff is still looking into me as a murder suspect."

"As far as I know."

When his cheeks turned crimson, I realized the answer was a resounding yes. "Adam! I didn't kill anyone!" Jumping to my feet, I began to pace. Maybe Darla had been right: I needed to reevaluate my relationship with Adam. If he didn't trust me enough to be certain I wasn't a killer...

"I know that!" he said, also standing and then grabbing my shoulders. "I never thought for a minute you had anything to do with Sylvia's death, Bernie."

Sincerity shone from his gaze. Biting my lip, I

crossed my arms over my chest. "Then why aren't you putting a stop to the sheriff's investigation?"

"I can't!" Adam threw his arms up in the air and strode across the small space. "When Walker gets an itch, he scratches it. Right now, you're on his list. He'll check out everything you said, then he'll take you off. His investigation methods are slow and methodical."

"Everything about Bruce is slow and methodical," Ruby said. "Now ask Adam where his stupid ghost is."

"I'm right here, Ruby." Ned appeared next to her. For some reason, his bloodstained shirt really bothered me even though I'd seen it dozens of times. Perhaps because I'd seen a lot of blood lately.

"About time, you old coot. I was beginning to think you didn't want me around."

Ned glanced at me and I shook my head. Ruby acted tough, but I had a feeling that her finding out the one other ghost we knew wanted to be left alone would devastate her.

"It's nice to see you," he said, his tone indicating he'd rather take a shot to the chest again than deal with Ruby.

"What's going on?" Adam asked.

"Nothing," I said, heaving a sigh of relief. "We can get back to discussing the investigation."

I took my seat on the couch and tried to remember Adam didn't think of me as a suspect—only the sheriff did. And that would be cleared up as soon as he pulled his head out of his—

"We're still working on getting fingerprints from the hammer," Adam said. "Shouldn't be too long."

Tina obviously hadn't been forthright with the police. Pursing my lips, I decided to share what I'd learned, even though it felt like I was throwing her under the bus. The police would have the answer eventually, so maybe revealing what I knew would speed up removing me from the suspect list... or at least bring me down a couple of pegs. "You'll find Tina's fingerprints all over it," I said. "She told me she picked it up when she found Sylvia's body because she recognized it as her own. I can verify it had been left out in the front garden overnight."

Adam stared at me a long moment, then shook his head while grabbing a pen and paper from a file folder on the coffee table. "Good to know."

"If Tina didn't kill her that morning, I think

someone grabbed the hammer from her house and went to knock Sylvia in the head."

"Maybe someone walking down the street in the early morning hours?"

I shrugged. "That would be Wilder."

With a nod, he took more notes. "What else have you found out?"

"Yolanda's glad she's gone... maybe a little too happy about it."

"Don't throw LaLa under the bus like that, Bernie!" Ruby yelled. "Don't be a snitch! Snitches get shanked!"

"Why do you say that?" Adam asked.

Ignoring Ruby, I replied, "Because she told me so. She's running around in the buff without a neighbor screaming at her to put on clothes." If also mentioning Yolanda's joy at Sylvia's demise meant me being dropped as a suspect, I didn't have a problem with it. Besides, I only spoke the truth. And, there wasn't any evidence Yolanda was involved, so I didn't really consider what I shared with Adam to be snitching.

He furrowed his brow. "I can't imagine someone killing another over fighting about clothing."

I shrugged. He was the cop, not me. I just provided the information.

Ruby strode over and hunched down in front of me. "Instead of sticking a knife in Yolanda's back, why don't you tell him about Sylvia's ex?"

Right. I'd almost forgotten about him. "Did you get an alibi for the ex-husband, Cody?" I asked, turning back to Adam.

He nodded. "Yes. Seems like a nice guy."

"Where was he?"

"At a coffee shop in Cottonwood he frequents regularly. We verified it with the barista and the owner."

Ruby stood and walked back over to Ned. "So, what's been shaking, stranger? If I didn't know any better, I'd say you've been avoiding me."

After clearing his throat, he replied, "It's been quiet around here. Actually, it's been very nice."

I tuned out the ghosts and focused on Adam. "Hopefully he won't get in trouble, but he was in Sylvia's house last night."

Adam arched an eyebrow. "Really? How do you know?"

I gave him the condensed version of how I met my new houseguest and explained she hoped Sylvia's spirt was trapped because she wanted to speak to her. "When she saw Cody's flashlight, she thought it may be Sylvia's ghost. She went over to talk to her, I followed, and we met Cody."

"That woman doesn't sound very stable, Bernie," Adam grumbled. "I wish she wasn't staying at your house."

"Well, I need the money. Besides, you and I both know ghosts *are* real and maybe Luna can see things I can't. I'm not going to judge her mental state."

The unearthly bickering between the two ghosts continued to make it difficult for me to concentrate on what Adam was saying. Sometimes, they were the best of friends, but not then. In fact, they reminded me of two toddlers arguing.

"I could've loaned you money," Adam muttered. "I'd be happy to. In fact, it wouldn't even be a loan. It would've been me bailing out the woman I love."

He'd only recently told me he loved me for the first time, but when I heard it, goosebumps still swept over my skin, butterflies tickled my belly, and my heart leapt into my throat. "You're so sweet," I murmured. "I love you, too."

We smiled at each other as Ned yelled, "Don't you ever shut up?"

Uh oh. I glanced over at the ghosts and almost fainted. Ruby had picked up a glass from the counter, her face contorted in rage as she flung it at Ned. Of course, it passed right through him and hit the wall.

As it shattered, I simply stared at my grandmother, absolutely stunned.

She wasn't supposed to be able to move inanimate objects.

CHAPTER 12

AT THAT POINT, I wasn't sure what to do. Adam and I jumped to our feet and stared in stunned silence at the broken shards. Ned disappeared and Ruby acted as if she'd just won the lottery and a bottle of tequila.

"Did... did Ned do that?" Adam finally whispered.

I shook my head. "It was Ruby."

"Did you see that?" she yelled. "Holy cow, what a pitch!"

"How?" Adam asked, slowly sitting down again. "She... she can't do stuff like that."

"I know."

What did it mean? What happened that suddenly gave Ruby the ability to interact with our world?

I felt sick. "I should go," I murmured, trying not to think about the scene. "I'll help you clean up, and we'll leave."

Ruby danced around the living room yelling for Ned again. "Hey, old timer! Come on out so I can practice my aim! Your cranky face is the perfect target!"

"Actually, I should just go," I sighed. "This is out of hand now."

With a nod, Adam took me in an embrace, his brow furrowed in worry and confusion. "Call me later."

As I drove home, Ruby giggled and chirped beside me.

"Things just became really interesting!" she said, bouncing in her seat. Unfortunately, she wasn't wrong.

"We need to lay some ground rules with this... this new ability," I said.

"I don't like rules," Ruby replied, crossing her arms over her chest. "They're no fun."

In her world, that may be the case, but she couldn't be hurling stuff around whenever she wanted.

After racing down my street and pulling into

the dirt lot behind my house, I killed the ignition and turned to my grandmother. "I understand, but we *need* rules, Ruby."

She rolled her eyes. "You practically advertise you have a ghost under your roof! Now I can really put on a show!"

I'd always played up the fact that my bed and breakfast was haunted, but that was based on reviewers who claimed to smell lavender and marijuana and wake up in the middle of the night with goosebumps. I never denied, nor had I confirmed, I had a ghost, even when I realized I did. Frankly, I'd felt fortunate she couldn't move inanimate objects because if there was one word to describe Ruby, it was unpredictable. In her former state, she was harmless. With this newfound ability, the last thing I needed was her throwing glasses at my customers or scaring them so badly my business flatlined, never to be revived again.

"Ruby, I'm afraid you're going to kill the bed and breakfast. It's one thing for someone to *think* they're staying in a haunted house; it's another thing for them to be physically hurt by flying objects."

She snickered and waved her hand between us, as if to brush away my concerns. "Oh, I'm not going to throw anything at anyone."

I only felt slightly better, and frankly, I had my doubts.

"Unless they make me mad. Then, I'll consider it."

With all my hopes of her behaving herself dashed to dust, I exited the car and headed inside.

After shedding my coat and hanging it up along with my purse, I glanced around the kitchen, looking for signs of my guest. Not even a glass in the sink. I walked through the living room and dining room and didn't find her.

"She's not up here!" Ruby yelled, appearing at the top of the steps. She disappeared into the Death Room, and I sighed, worried about what she was doing. Probably moving all of Luna's things around. A headache began to form behind my eyes as I sat on the couch.

Instead of concentrating on the chaos Ruby was most likely causing—and what had changed to give her the ability to do so—I thought about my next move. The only one of my neighbors I hadn't spoken to after the murder was Pete. And neither had the police. He'd mentioned how much he'd been working, and Adam had revealed they'd tried to catch up with him a couple of times. They'd finally agreed to meet at the sheriff's office in two days.

I stood and glanced out the window. Behind the huge Palo Verde, Pete's truck stood in the driveway. With Ruby upstairs, I could sneak out undetected and with the knowledge she wouldn't be able to toss anything in Pete's house.

After slipping out the front door, I hurried away from my home. I glanced behind me, half expecting to find her following me. Thankfully, it seemed her inability to leave the house without me remained intact. Thank goodness for small favors.

What the heck would I say to Pete, though? I needed to appear friendly and make him want to share any knowledge about the murder with me. I had a knack for gathering information. People said things to me they didn't share with the police. As I approached his driveway, I deliberated continuing my walk until I got my thoughts together. I glanced up to find him sitting on his porch, beer in hand. He smiled and motioned for me to join him.

Dang it. I'd have to wing it. Going in without a solid plan... the story of my life.

I smiled and headed up the driveway. A saw lay against the huge tree. "Are you getting ready to trim it?"

He chuckled and shook his head. "I'm

thinking about it. Part of me is ready to trim it since she's gone, the other part of me wants to keep it the way it is to spite her. But, at least I got the saw out."

A table and a set of chairs barely fit on the small porch. I took the other seat and he pointed to the cooler at his feet. "Beer?"

I nodded. It had been quite the day and my stress levels were through the roof worrying about Ruby's potential antics.

After popping open the can, I took a long drink and tried to cover the belch with something I hoped resembled a cough.

Pete chuckled. "Not much of a beer drinker, are you?"

"Sorry, no." I kept my gaze on the street until the heat in my cheeks diminished.

"Don't worry about it," Pete said. "Everyone burps."

I turned to him and smiled, ready to change the subject to anything but my gastrointestinal system. "How're you doing?"

He shrugged. "Fine. No one's hassling me, work is going good. I don't have any complaints."

I glanced down at the tool chest next to the cooler. A hammer protruded from the half-closed case. The rubber grip appeared to be worn, part of it missing. Hmm... interesting.

"How long did you and Sylvia have an affair?" I asked, jumping in with both feet.

"Not long," he replied, shaking his head. "I didn't know she was married. When I found out, that was it. I don't date married women. I'm not a homewrecker."

Usually, the term 'homewrecker' was saved for women participating in out-of-marriage dalliances, and I found it interesting Pete described himself in that way.

"Did you ever meet her husband?"

He shook his head. "No. But during our breakup, she explained her husband was awful, and she was trying to get out of the marriage. She said his whole family was terrible. His father had been abusive to him, and his mother had run, taking him and his brother with her. The father had tried to hunt them down... Sylvia's husband had dysfunction at every turn growing up and it made him mean. She was waiting for the right time to leave him... said she was afraid of what he'd do when she did."

"Like what?" I asked.

"She feared he'd become violent with her."

I took another sip of beer, listening intently.

"Her sob story apparently didn't soften your stance on extra-marital affairs."

"No, it didn't. I watched my father have sidepiece after sidepiece and how it ate away at my mother. Each time, a little slice of her died. I didn't want to be responsible for doing that to someone."

I sighed and sat back in my chair. "How did you two end it?" I asked. "Did you want to see her after she left her husband?"

Pete took a long pull from his beer can, then crushed it and set it down next to his chair. "Because of my past, I have very little tolerance for things like that. Even if her marriage was that awful, it didn't mean she wouldn't do it again with someone in the future. I didn't want to be that someone." He chuckled as he opened another can. "I guess a therapist would say I have some trust issues, which is why I've never been married before. At the first sign of trouble, I'm out the door."

I understood his stance, but what a difficult way to live. I tried to imagine always searching for clues of infidelity or malice in a relationship. It would become exhausting for both parties involved: the accused and the accuser.

The contradiction between the way Sylvia described her husband and the man I'd encountered was astounding. Perhaps he'd been playing the suffering ex-husband who couldn't get over his wife when we'd met. If that were the case, he was dang good at it. An expert manipulator.

"I met her ex," I said. "He was in her house the other night."

Pete's eyes widened. "Are you kidding me?"

"No. It's a long story, but I ended up going over there. He said he just wanted to be close to her. That he was devastated she was gone."

"That doesn't match with the guy Sylvia described," Pete replied, narrowing his gaze. "I wonder which one's the liar?"

"I have no idea," I said, shrugging.

After another long pull of beer, he set down his can. "Do you think he could've done it?"

"No."

"Why not?"

How did I reveal the information without giving away the fact Adam had entrusted me with investigational evidence? "It's my understanding he's got an alibi."

"Where did you hear that? Your boyfriend?"

I smiled. "My sources are confidential. If I revealed them, I'd have to kill you."

Pete laughed and pointed at the toolbox. "You

got a hammer right there. Are you going to do me in Sylvia-style?"

We both chuckled at the inappropriate remark, and I stood. "I need to head home." I wasn't about to explain I had to figure out how to corral my wild ghost. "Thanks for the beer."

"Anytime, Bernie. Have a good one."

As I hurried home, my thoughts returned to Ruby's new ability. She and I had guessed that ghosts became stronger the longer they'd been trapped between here and their final resting place. For instance, Ned had been dead at least ninety years longer than Ruby, if not a full century. He could move things around and often played games with Adam, like hiding his shoes or important documents, which was why my boyfriend had installed the camera in his condo.

Ruby had been gone for about four years now and was throwing glasses at other ghosts. Our theory of being dead longer equaling stronger ghostly abilities had been trounced to dust.

At my front door, I took a deep breath and shut my eyes for a moment. When I opened them, my ghost stood at the window glaring at me, a red and brown throw pillow from the couch in her hand. She shook her head, obviously angry, then walked away. I'd annoyed her by leaving without her.

Frankly, I wasn't just worried about Ruby inadvertently ruining my business while she had her fun terrorizing my guests. I was also petrified she'd soon be able to leave me.

CHAPTER 13

When I walked in the door, Ruby slammed me over the head with the pillow.

"Ow!" I yelled, turning to her. "That hurt!"

She cackled and smacked me again, this time directly in the face. "This is your punishment for leaving me here! You didn't even ask me if I wanted to go!"

Before she hit me the third time, I grabbed it out of her hand and held it above my head while she jumped for it, unable to reach it. "What do you think of that, short stuff?" I twisted and turned as her cold hands brushed against me, sending goosebumps down my spine.

"Give me that!" she shouted as I laughed.

"No! Get it yourself you—"

"Is everything okay?"

Uh oh.

I glanced over at the open door to find Wilder and Luna staring at us. Well, me. They were staring at me, while I held a pillow over my head and laughed as I danced around. I must have looked ridiculous.

Ruby burst out into giggles and stepped away. "How are you going to get out of this one?"

The two stared at me, concern shining from their gazes. How did I explain a pillow fight with a ghost?

I didn't.

Instead, I threw the pillow in the air, made some noise that I hope sounded like laughter, then caught it. "I love this thing!" I said, holding it close to my chest. "It's a great pillow. So comfortable, yet supportive, when I use it against my lower back while sitting on the couch! It's my favorite in the house! And I have a lot of pillows in here!"

Luna and Wilder exchanged glances but remained quiet, Ruby's laughter being the only sound.

I smiled and tossed the pillow, then caught it, once again. "You have to celebrate the wonderful, little things in life, right?" It was then I realized that Wilder and Luna were together. At my house. "Do you two know each other?"

Wilder's eyes lit up and he gazed at Luna with unabashed love. "We met this morning."

"This morning?"

"Yes. I saw him out walking and I was pulled to him. I had to meet him, so I ran out and introduced myself."

"It was the best moment of my life," Wilder sighed as he wrapped his arm around her. "I've found my other half. The craft to my witch."

"What does that mean?" I asked.

"We both practice witchcraft," Luna said. "Our meeting must have been fated."

Ruby crossed her arms over her chest. "Wait a hot minute. They met… hours ago and they're all lovey-dovey?"

"I think Wilder was why I felt like I was summoned here," Luna said as they stared into each other's eyes. "He's my everything."

Although I found it hard to believe the nonsense dribbling from their mouths, I couldn't tear my gaze away from Wilder's forearm. A tattoo I'd never noticed before—a blue, five-point star—caught my attention and seemed to shine brighter than anything I'd seen at night.

"Everything okay, Bernie?" Wilder asked. "You

look a little pale." He pulled his arm away from Luna and yanked down his shirt sleeve.

I smiled. "Fine. Yes. Everything's fine."

"Which means it's not," Ruby interjected. "What's up, Bernie?"

"We came by to get Luna's things," Wilder continued. "She's going to be moving in with me."

My heart thundered as I smiled and nodded. Even though I would miss the woman's nightly payment, I couldn't wait to get the house to myself. I might have just discovered a clue to the murderer. "Well, don't let me celebrating my wonderful pillow stop you!" They once again traded a glance as I shut the front door. "I'll be in the kitchen if you need me!"

I hurried through the dining room and into the kitchen, my cheeks burning with embarrassment at the situation. If it hadn't been for Ruby, I wouldn't have been caught in such an uncomfortable spot.

After grabbing a glass of water, I sat at the kitchen island and pulled out my phone.

"What're you doing?" Ruby asked from behind me.

"Shh," I whispered. "I'm mad at you."

"That's okay. You can still tell me what you're up to."

I spun around on the stool. "This is going to sound crazy, but I'm wondering if Wilder had something to do with the murder."

"Why do you think that?"

Even though I heard Wilder and Luna upstairs, I glanced through Ruby to make sure we were alone. "Do you remember how we found Sylvia?"

"I'm not sure what you're getting at," Ruby said. "We found her when Tina started screaming."

"But do you remember how she looked?"

Ruby nodded. "Dead."

With a sigh, I rolled my eyes. "What else?"

"She was spread-eagle."

I stared at her, hoping she'd put the pieces together. When she furrowed her brow and shrugged, I wondered if my imagination had gone into overdrive. "Did you think she... she had been placed like that?"

"Well, I certainly don't think she died in the position," Ruby said. "My guess is that she'd been stretched out. It didn't look natural."

"I agree," I murmured, now excited. "In fact, she resembled a star."

Ruby sighed. "Can you please explain this to me?"

I slid off the stool and went around the island to my junk drawer where I pulled out a pen and paper. I drew the star, then made an outline of what I hoped mirrored the way we'd found Sylvia.

"Oh, yes. I see the similarities. Apparently, I'm a very visual person," Ruby said, nodding. "But I still don't get it."

The familiar creaks and moans of people coming down the stairs caught my attention and I hurried through the dining room and into the living room.

"Thanks for letting me stay," Luna said. "I love your home."

"I'm glad you took her in as well," Wilder chimed. "If you hadn't, we may never have met."

The star on his arm glared at me as if it had been placed in a spotlight. "Well, I'm glad..." For what? That I may be sending Luna home with a killer?

"We'll see you later, Bernie!" Wilder said. "Talk to you soon."

Ruby snorted as they walked out. "I see that lasting about six seconds shy of one hot minute."

I raced back into the kitchen, grabbed my phone, and pulled up Google.

What did the star represent, if anything?

After finding an article claiming to have been written by a practicing witch, I settled in to read.

THE PENTAGRAM IS ORIGINALLY from ancient Sumerian and represented the human Physical and Elemental form. The physical form consists of head, two arms and two legs, with elemental symbolism being Earth, Fire, Air and Water. See the drawing below for representation.

"ALL THAT DOESN'T SEEM like it would lead to a murder," Ruby said from over my shoulder. "Seems pretty harmless." I studied the sketch of the man, each one of his appendages and his head assigned an element. Ruby was right. It didn't seem to link to a killer at all. With a sigh, I continued reading.

IN THE 20ᵀᴴ CENTURY, Hollywood adopted the Pentagram as a sign of devil worshipping and evil. Many today who practice Satanism use the pentagram upside down to denote their beliefs.

. . .

"WAS THAT UPSIDE DOWN?" I asked. "I can't remember."

"Don't know."

I stared out the kitchen window and pondered what I'd learned. Wilder made teas and salves for a living and seemed to be one of the kindest, quietest people I'd ever met. At the neighborhood meeting, he'd said, *I'm not very good with confrontation. I prefer to live peacefully.* That didn't jive with devil worshipping for me. I attempted to imagine him wearing horns and sacrificing goats. Or maybe devil worshippers only did that in the movies. I was so far out of my realm of knowledge, I may as well have been in a different universe.

Ruby walked around the island and stood directly in my line of sight. "What're you thinking?"

"What if Wilder is a Satan worshipper? What if he walked down the street that morning and decided he needed to make some sort of sacrifice?"

"Wouldn't he do that with a goat or a chicken?"

I shrugged. "I don't know anything about Satanism, and that's one rabbit hole I don't want to stick my nose into."

"Don't blame you on that one."

We sat in silence for a few moments, then a horrible thought curdled my stomach. "Ruby, what if Wilder does practice some evil religion and he killed Sylvia, and Luna's next?"

Her eyes widened. "Oh, my goodness. That means we sent her packing with a psychopath!"

Well, she *left* with a psychopath, but potato, pot-ah-to. "What do we do? Should we call the police?"

Ruby tapped her bottom lip. "No. If we're letting our imaginations get the best of us, then you've made an enemy of him if the police show up at his house. If he's the killer, you're going to be next."

"And what if he's hurting Luna?"

"Well, let's go check it out."

"What do you want to do? Go sneak around his house and look in the windows?"

"Yes," she replied with a shrug. "What did you want to do? Slide down his chimney like Santa?"

"Well, I certainly don't want to slink around his property. He probably owns a gun." I read somewhere that almost fifty percent of the people in Arizona were gun owners. I'd seen a few carrying at the grocery store. Even though Wilder was a peace-loving herbal tea maker, I had a fifty-

fifty chance he was one who did, and I didn't want to be shot.

But Wilder was walking by Sylvia's that morning. She'd called it into the police herself. He also had access to the hammer Tina had left in her front yard. And, he may or may not be a devil worshipper, which was also troubling.

Another thought suddenly occurred to me. "Ruby, don't you think it's weird that Luna showed up like she did? With all her talk of being "summoned," that she felt a "pull," and now she's shacked up with Wilder after only meeting him a few hours ago?"

"I do think she's a strange one," Ruby agreed.

"What if… what if she's in on it? What if she and Wilder are some sort of maniacal murdering duo?"

"Oh, that sounds like a great slasher movie," Ruby said. "The Maniacal Murdering Duo."

"What do you think?"

Ruby sighed and paced around the kitchen island, her hands behind her back as she stared at the floor. Finally, she looked at me. "I think you may have a very legitimate question. We need to find out more about Lunatic Luna."

CHAPTER 14

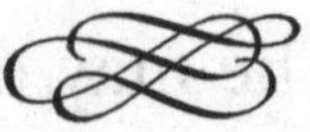

THE NEXT MORNING, I walked over to Wilder's house with Ruby in tow. My hand shook as I knocked on the door, but I pasted a smile on my face, hoping I didn't appear scared, but instead, friendly.

"Bernie!" he greeted me. "What can I do for you?"

I swallowed past the anxiety I'd built up. But at least I had a plan to scope out his place—well, Ruby would do the spying—and didn't have to wing it with my reasoning for being there. "I... I was wondering about your teas."

His kind, reassuring smile eased my nervousness. "Sure. Come on in and let's discuss what's going on with you and what can be done."

"They said Ted Bundy had a nice smile just like this guy," Ruby said. "Watch your back or you're going to end up buzzard breakfast in the desert."

Wonderful.

I smiled as I followed him in, half-expecting to find Luna laid out in the living room with her head bashed in.

Ruby was ahead of me, peeking into every nook and cranny she could. As we passed the hallway, she started down that way, but was quickly jerked back toward me as I trailed Wilder into the living room. Two brown Barcaloungers sat facing each other with a small table in between. A worn, brown and red area rug covered the hardwood floors. The walls had been painted a calming taupe color and plants sat on shelves lining the wall where the television should've been.

"Those are pot plants," Ruby said, pointing at them. "Doesn't surprise me that Wilder enjoys a bit of the ganga."

As he motioned for me to sit in one of the loungers, I glanced into the dining room. Small bags and tins arranged neatly in rows covered a large, oval wooden table, sans chairs. "Is that your store?" I asked, pointing.

He nodded as he sat down. "Yes. Specialty teas and salves." His voice beamed with pride. "What's on your mind today, Bernie?"

I'd given a lot of thought to what ailment I would suggest I needed treated. Anxiety seemed to be the easiest and most encompassing, not to mention the most prevalent. "I tend to suffer from a bit of anxiety."

Ruby snorted and shook her head. "A bit? You're wound tighter than a straight boy's butt cheeks in prison."

I gave her a quick glare, then concentrated on Wilder.

"Anxiety can be rough," Wilder said. "I won't ask you what sets you off. I know it's different for every person. Sometimes, it's the big things, sometimes it's the small things that seem insignificant to others. I would, however, suggest that you journal about it and find your triggers."

"Everything," Ruby said. "Everything sets you off."

Wilder furrowed his brow. "Do you sleep well?"

"Every now and then," I said with a shrug.

"After you've worn yourself out with anxiety," Ruby chimed in.

What she mentioned was true, but I wished

she'd shut up. This would be so much easier without her commentary.

"I'll get you some tea samples that I think will help," Wilder said, standing. "You can try them and let me know your thoughts."

I stood and walked around the living room, giving Ruby a chance to explore beyond its boundaries.

"Nothing in the hall closet," she called. "Ask him where Luna is, though. Why hasn't Lunatic Luna shown herself? And come this way so I can look down the hall."

I strolled over to the hallway and pretended to study a three-foot-high table holding candles, a few wilted flowers, and some other little knick-knacks I didn't recognize. In the middle of it lay a picture of Sylvia.

Why in the world would he have a picture of Sylvia on the little table?

My heart thundered as I glanced over my shoulder. Wilder was picking through the inventory in the dining room with his back to me. I leaned over and studied the display more closely, then picked up the photo.

It had been taken without her knowledge. She was in her car, driving down our street, passing Wilder's house. He must have either snapped it from inside through the window or was standing outside near the front door. Glancing over at the glass pane, I noted a few streaks and some dust. The picture seemed clear and pristine, so he must have been outside.

Was it part of the devil worshipping? Was the table some type of altar where he placed his offerings to Satan? I glanced around for a picture of Luna but didn't see one.

I set down the photo and turned back toward the living room. Wilder smiled as he approached. Studying his face, I searched for evil intent, but saw none. Yet, my anxiety caught the breath in my throat. Was I face-to-face with a killer? I had to play it cool, not let him know I was on to him.

"Try this," he said, handing me a small paper bag as my cheeks heated with fear. "There's some lavender, chamomile, and catnip in there. See which one works best. Or, if you like, I can make you a specialty blend with all three."

I glanced in the bag at the labeled teabags. "C-Catnip? I thought that was for cats."

"It's great for relaxation," he said.

"You better keep Elvira away from that," Ruby said. "She'll tear that up in no time."

I pulled out a small tin no bigger than a half-dollar. "What's this?" Some devil juice that submitted my soul to Satan when I used it?

"A lavender salve I made. You may want to dab a little on your temples and wrists before bed. It'll help you relax."

How did a man who made tea and salves become a devil worshipper? I just didn't see it. Instead of assuming things and allowing my imagination to go wild, I pointed to the altar and asked, "Why do you have a picture of Sylvia?"

I mean, I had been taking self-defense classes for months. I stepped away and placed most of my weight on my back foot. If need be, I'd take down the herb-loving killer and solve this case.

"We're getting ready to rumble!" Ruby yelled. She hurried over to a bookcase behind Wilder and picked up the largest tome available—a dictionary of herbs. "I'll smack this guy into next week if I need to!"

My job was now not only to protect myself but keep Wilder's attention on me so he didn't see the floating book behind him. I appreciated Ruby's desire to help me, but she also added another layer of concern to the situation.

He ran a hand over his beard and sighed. "As I told you, I practice witchcraft. When Sylvia threatened to have my store shut down, I placed a protective spell on myself and my house."

"A spell?" Ruby asked. "If he's going to go all hocus-pocus, why not just put a spell on Sylvia to get run over by a bus?"

Or hit on the head with a hammer.

"Did you…" How to word it delicately… "Did you put a spell on her so something bad would happen?"

Wilder gasped and took two steps backward, almost running into Ruby and the book. She yelped and jumped out of the way while Wilder's brow furrowed in disbelief. "Of course not. A witch doesn't wish harm on people. My spells are all positive energy. I choose to protect myself instead of causing injury to those who want to hurt me." Based on his glare and the tone of his voice, I'd obviously offended him.

Ruby set the book down, then walked over to him, hands on hips. "Ask him where Luna is. I don't believe his good witch act. He's probably buried her in the backyard."

"Where's Luna?" I asked.

"Why?"

"Because I want to make sure she's okay," I said, my voice stronger than my shaky hands and trembling knees made me out to be.

While Wilder stared at me as if I were out of my mind, I took a few steps toward the front door, ready to make my escape.

"Do you think I killed Sylvia?" he finally asked. "That I'm some type of lunatic serial killer who goes around collecting women to murder?"

Well, yes. That exact thought had crossed my mind. A devil worshipping lunatic serial killer. "Where is she?"

"In the bedroom, asleep. She didn't get a good night's rest at your place because she said it smelled like weed and lavender and she got the chills multiple times so bad, they woke her."

"He drugged her!" Ruby shouted. "He's drugged her and then he's going to chop her up into little pieces and—"

"Luna said she thinks your place is haunted," Wilder continued. "Says she can feel a spirit in your house."

Well, she wasn't wrong. Ruby finally stopped yelling and twirled around in a circle with her arms out to her sides, cackling. "Booga! Booga! Booga!" she yelled. "I'm *so* scary!" She picked up the dictionary again and held it over her head as if she were really going to smack Wilder.

I needed to get her out of there, but I also wanted to be sure Luna was okay. "Let me see her. If you've got nothing to hide, I want to see Luna."

He shook his head. "You're unbelievable. You come here with some nonsense about anxiety and now you're practically accusing me of being a serial killer?"

"Her anxiety isn't nonsense," Ruby yelled. "I ought to knock you out, bubba!"

"How did all this start?" Wilder asked. "Why in the world would you think of me like this?"

I refused to admit that a stupid tattoo had sent me into a downward spiral of wondering if he was a devil worshipper.

"I think it's best you leave my home before I call the police," Wilder said, pointing to the front door. "To get rid of all your negative juju, I'm not even going to charge you for the tea. Just please, go."

"How rude," Ruby muttered, setting down the book.

Even though I still hadn't seen Luna, I decided it would be best if the police weren't involved. I glanced around, looking for any indication that my former guest had been hurt and was not tucked away in the back room, sound asleep. I found none.

Wilder walked over to the door and opened it.

He didn't meet my gaze as I marched past him, my head held high.

"Bye, killer," Ruby muttered. "We're going to put you away."

"And Bernie?" Wilder called. "Please don't come back. I'll be forced to get a restraining order. I can't have your negativity near me."

"That seems a little over the top," I muttered.

"I agree," Ruby said. "Restraining orders are fun, though."

"What does that mean?"

"Well, say he gets one declaring that you can't go within fifteen feet of him. You follow him around town, staying exactly fifteen feet away. It drives them nuts."

"And I take it you know this from experience?"

"I plead the fifth."

Of course my grandmother would be familiar with all the ins and outs of restraining orders. How many had been lodged against her while she was alive?

Once I reached my house, I tossed the bag on the kitchen island and sat down in one of the stools. Elvira came out from my bedroom and quickly jumped onto the counter to smell the bag. I didn't even have the energy to shoo her off.

"I think he did it," Ruby said. "Why wouldn't he show us Luna? What's he hiding?"

Elvira pawed at the bag and meowed.

"She wants that catnip," Ruby muttered. "Your cat's a druggie."

As the feline batted around the paper bag, my thoughts remained on Wilder. Why hadn't he retrieved Luna? If he had, I wouldn't have considered him a suspect in the murder. But the fact that he hadn't worried me... not only for Luna's safety, but now for my own.

CHAPTER 15

ADAM ARRIVED for dinner right on time and I asked him to go knock on Wilder's door. After explaining my concerns, he shook his head and plopped down on a kitchen stool. He wasn't going anywhere.

"Bernie, I can't go over to his house in any official capacity. Luna went with him willingly and you said there was no sign of foul play. I'm sure she's fine."

"She's probably six feet under in the back-yard," Ruby muttered.

"What if you went over in a non-official capacity?" I asked. "Please? He's got a dang altar with Sylvia's picture on it! He could be a serial killer, Adam."

"And he could be a guy who sells teas and needs to trim his beard. I saw the altar. He explained it was used to cast spells to protect himself from her."

"You believed that?"

"I have no reason not to," Adam said, shrugging. "It's a little unconventional, yes, but to each their own. I know enough about Wicca to know I don't know much."

I really felt it needed to be investigated further, especially since I hadn't seen Luna. "Please?" I bat my eyelashes at him and ran my fingers through his hair. "Pretty please? I won't be able to calm down until I know she's okay."

"What's wrong?" he asked. "Do you have something in your eye?"

I slapped him and placed my hands on my hips. "Adam! Just go to Wilder's and make sure everything's okay! See if Luna's there!"

"Why don't you go?" he asked.

I had mentioned I'd been there earlier in the day, but I'd omitted Wilder's threat of the restraining order.

With a sigh, I shook my head, then pulled a five-dollar bill out of my pocket and handed it to Adam. "Tell him you want some chamomile tea."

"Ugh," Ruby said. "Horrible, nasty stuff."

Wilder knew I dated Adam, so I hoped he wouldn't mention my earlier visit. Adam would be upset I had meddled to the point of being threatened with a restraining order.

I smiled as Adam stood. There wouldn't be any more catnip tea coming into the house. I'd stuffed the bag into a drawer earlier and Elvira had sat on the floor and stared at it for an hour, her tail swishing. Dang junkie.

"Fine," Adam said. "Only for you."

"I'll get dinner ready," I said, standing on my tiptoes and giving him a quick kiss on the cheek.

"Sounds good."

As the front door shut, I hurried into the kitchen. Me getting dinner ready consisted of opening the Mexican takeout boxes he'd brought and a bottle of wine.

"I'll leave you two," Ruby said, her gaze resting wistfully on my plate. "Those tacos look delicious."

I smiled as she faded away, then set the plates on the dining room table. When I heard the front door open, I hurried into the living room to find Adam with a paper bag.

"Here's your tea," he said, handing it to me.

"Did you see her?"

He shook his head.

"You didn't find Luna?"

"No. Just Wilder. He mentioned you'd visited earlier in the day."

I waited for the lecture on how it was wrong to blatantly accuse people of murder without any hard evidence, but it never came.

"Dang, those tacos look amazing," he continued as his stomach growled loud enough for me to hear. "Let's chow down."

I took a seat. "Maybe a movie after dinner?" I asked. Since meeting Adam, who adored movies, I'd added a bunch of subscription services and had so much television available, I could never get through all of it even if I never did anything but sit in front of the screen.

"That sounds great. What are you in the mood for?"

"Maybe a drama. Or a comedy. I'm not sure. Let's see what we've got available."

Once I'd stuffed my face with too many tacos, Adam and I did the dishes, working together efficiently as if we'd been living together for years. Then, he pulled two bowls out of the cabinet, found the silverware drawer in one try, and scooped us out some ice cream. It was then I realized just how much time he spent at my house when he wasn't investigating a murder. He moved about as if it were his own, knowing where everything was stashed.

"Why are you staring at me like that?" he asked, wiggling his eyebrows at me. "You like what you see?"

"Of course I do." What was there not to like? Blond hair, blue eyes, nice build... maybe I'd like to see even more of him. "Have you ever thought about us moving in together?"

He set down the scooper and handed me a bowl. "Yes, I have."

"Do you think it would be a good idea?" I couldn't look at him. Instead, I kept my gaze focused firmly on my chocolate chunk cookie dough ice cream. Perhaps I was deeper into this relationship than he was, and I wasn't prepared to face that fact.

"It's a big step."

Wishing the floor would swallow me up, I nodded as my cheeks heated. He wasn't ready. I should've realized that. Think before you speak was always a good rule to live by.

"But, yes, I think it's something we should discuss."

My ice cream caught in my throat and I began

to cough. A chunk of cookie dough flew across the space between us and landed on his chest. As I sputtered to catch my breath, he set down his bowl and tapped between my shoulder blades. "Do I need to do the Heimlich?" he asked, his brow furrowed in concern. "Are you okay, Bernie?"

With a nod, I held out my hand, hoping he wouldn't grab me from behind. "I just need to catch my breath," I wheezed.

Having imagined this situation, I'd always fantasized it would be romantic. Not me sending bits of cookie dough onto his clothing.

He smiled and stepped back, then glanced down at his shirt. Without a word, he wiped up the mess I'd made.

Once I could breathe again, I smiled at him. "That was messy."

"Life is like that sometimes," he said with a chuckle, taking me in an embrace.

And it was. Whether it was me trying to solve a murder or spewing ice cream like the possessed girl in the Exorcist, life was full of twists and turns... and messiness.

"Would you want to live here?" I asked.

He nodded. "I think so. It seems silly to give up this big, beautiful house for a condo."

"How do you feel about living in a bed and breakfast, though?"

"I don't think it'll be a problem. What about Ruby? What do you think she'll have to say?"

"Well, I'm not sure her opinion counts."

He shrugged and glanced around. "She lives here, too."

I sighed with frustration. My life wasn't going to be put on hold because Ruby didn't want Adam to move in. I couldn't imagine her attempting to sway my decision about something so important, but one never knew what went through Ruby's mind. "Do we need to check with Ned as well?" Even to my own ears, my voice sounded snotty.

"Hey, don't be upset," Adam said, placing his hands on my shoulders. "It's a huge change, and unfortunately, there are four people involved instead of two. We'll work it out."

"Ghosts," I said. "Two people and two ghosts." I hated to say it, but I believed the people's opinion mattered more than the spirits'.

"You're right," he said with a laugh. "I love you, Bernie, and I do want to move in with you. I was actually considering bringing it up, but I didn't know if you were thinking along the same lines as me. I'm glad you do, and I'm looking forward to taking the next step in our relationship."

Did that mean marriage? Or maybe we'd wait to see if we could live together. One step at a time. Adam and I loved each other enough to attempt to share a home, and right now, that was good enough for me.

A knock sounded at the back door. It had to be friends—customers always came through the front, and lately, they'd been in short supply.

When I opened the door, Darlene and Jack smiled at me. I hadn't seen or heard from either one since Darlene's outburst about Adam.

"Hi," she said, her voice quiet and shy. "Can we come in?" I nodded and stepped aside. "Adam's here," she continued. "Perfect."

Was she being sincere or facetious? I couldn't really tell.

"I'm glad to see you both," she said once we'd gathered in the kitchen, her gaze darting between us as she tucked a lock of long blonde hair behind her ear. "First, Adam, I wanted to apologize to you for what I said the other day. I know you have a very important job to do and that you care very much about Bernie. It must be hard being caught between the sheriff and your girlfriend."

Adam leaned against the counter and nodded. "Yes, it is. Thank you for realizing that."

Darla smiled, seemingly encouraged by

Adam's reaction. "We all know Bernie had nothing do with the murder across the street, regardless of what the sheriff thinks. I'm sorry I got so angry."

"It's okay," Adam said. "I understand. You wanted to help your friend and I appreciate that. But like you said, I'm just in a difficult position. We need to check all our boxes, cross our T's... we have to be very thorough in a murder investigation."

"I get it and I shouldn't have reacted the way I did," Darla said, taking Jack's hand.

Jack glanced from me to Adam. "Are we all good?"

Both Adam and I nodded.

"Excellent," Jack said, beaming. "We have some news for both of you."

I was practically brimming with excitement to share my own announcement of Adam and me moving in together, but as Darla's cheeks turned pink, I held my breath. She looked as if she may simply explode with happiness.

"Jack and I are getting married!" she shouted. I stared in disbelief as she thrust her hand in my direction to reveal a rose gold band with a small, round diamond perched on top. As I took her hand in mine, she squealed.

"That's fantastic news," Adam said, shaking Jack's hand. "Congratulations!"

"I'm so happy for you," I whispered, hugging my friend. My news seemed so inconsequential, I didn't bother to share it and ruin Darla's moment.

"Thank you!" she said. "I can't believe how happy I am!"

As always, a little thread of worry tugged at me. Were her medications working as they should? Was she in a manic state, or was she truly this excited? I found nothing but sheer joy as I studied her face.

"I was hoping you'd be my maid of honor," she said.

The last wedding I'd attended—my cousin's— I'd been hit by lightning. Hopefully things would go much smoother this time. "I'd be delighted."

"And I'd like you to be my best man," Jack said, grinning at Adam.

"Wouldn't miss it, buddy."

"Did I hear Mr. Dimples?" Ruby said, appearing in the kitchen archway. "Well, I most certainly did. How's it going, hot stuff?"

"He's getting married," I said.

Ruby grimaced. "Dang it! I was hoping I'd wait around here long enough to snag him when he kicked the bucket!"

"What did she say?" Darla asked.

"She's very happy for you," I replied.

"She's welcome to come to the ceremony as well," Darla whispered. "If you want her there."

"I heard that!" Ruby yelled. "I may be dead, but I'm not deaf, sweetheart!"

"Where are you thinking of having the ceremony?" I asked.

"We found this really cute town up north a ways," Jack answered. He placed his arm over Darla's shoulder and pulled her close.

"It's like someone carved out a portion of the forest and set down this place. There's a river running through it, huge pine trees everywhere, little stores... it's gorgeous."

"What's it called?" Adam asked.

"Heywood," Jack said. "Prettiest place on Earth, I guarantee it.""

So when's the big day?" Adam asked.

"This summer," Darla said firmly.

"A couple of months away?" I asked. How in the world would she plan a wedding in such a short time period?

"Yes. We're keeping it small and simple. My parents, obviously our friends... we figure the guest list will be under thirty people."

I noticed how she hadn't mentioned anyone

from Jack's past. Had he shared with her that he used to be a professional burglar and done prison time? Hopefully, yes. Either that or it would come back to bite him at some point in the future.

"Will you go dress shopping with me?" Darla asked.

"Of course!"

"Oh, I love weddings!" Ruby sighed. "I can't wait!"

I didn't bother to mention I hadn't decided if she'd be attending. A getaway with Adam—*alone*—would be nice.

When his phone rang, the chatter immediately died and we all stared at him. After pulling out the device, he grimaced and swore under his breath. "I need to take this."

He hurried into the living room and I strained to overhear what he said as well as listen to Darla's wedding plans. Something about a little church overlooking the river...

"I need to go," Adam said. "That was the sheriff. He's got firm physical evidence on who killed Sylvia, and we're going to make an arrest."

"Who is it?" I asked.

"They're coming for you!" Ruby wailed, throwing her hands up in the air. "You're going down for this one!"

"Sorry, even though I love you, I can't tell you that," he said. With a wink, he waved goodbye and headed out the front door.

He wouldn't tell me he loved me if he was coming to arrest me... right?

CHAPTER 16

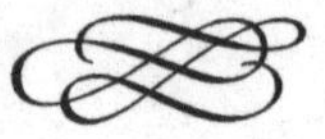

TWO HOURS LATER, when they brought Pete out of his house in handcuffs, I stood in the street with Yolanda and Tina watching the red and blue police lights illuminate the neighborhood. Pete yelled he was innocent and fought the cops as they dragged him from his house. He continued screaming until they stuffed him in the back of the cruiser and slammed the door.

"I feel so much safer now," Tina murmured, shaking her head. "What a horrible tragedy to take place on our quiet little street."

Yolanda nodded. "I agree. Pete seems fairly harmless, but the worst of them often do."

As I stared at the crescent moon, something didn't feel right. Yes, Pete had suggested Tina drop dead the evening before she was killed, and she'd relentlessly hassled him about his stupid tree. He'd had an affair with her. He had motive and opportunity, but what was the physical evidence Adam had mentioned?

And I still hadn't laid eyes on Luna. Where was Wilder? Why wasn't he outside watching his neighbor being hauled off to jail? More strange behavior from him.

"Has anyone seen Wilder and his new girlfriend?" I asked, still wondering if Luna was happily shacked up with him, or the cops had arrested the wrong man and he was planting rose bushes over her buried corpse.

Both shook their heads. "What new girlfriend?" Tina asked. "I hardly ever see any women over there."

"Yes," Yolanda said, pulling her sweater tighter around her thin frame. "Dish the dirt! What new girlfriend?"

I explained Luna staying with me and her and Wilder meeting, then her moving in with him. Probably best to omit the threat of a restraining order, though.

"How interesting," Tina said. "To invite someone into your home after only just making their acquaintance."

It wasn't much different than what I did, but I ran a business where strangers were supposed to stay in my house—and pay me well for it. And, I didn't have tattoos that strongly resembled symbols of what some may call devil worshipping, nor did I have an altar in my house featuring a picture of a murder victim.

Speaking of my non-existent business... despite the late hour, I had to attend to it, or I'd be out on my butt. Trying to imagine me, Ruby, Ned, and Adam living together in his small condo only reinforced the idea I needed to get my marketing machine rolling and also hire a lawyer for that stupid tax bill. I'd put it off long enough. Time to be an adult.

After leaving my neighbors, I grabbed my laptop from my bedroom and sat down at the kitchen island. Glancing over the events coming to Sedona in the coming weeks and months, I sent a few emails to organizers. Right around the corner, one of the local psychics was hosting a weekend crystal workshop. To my utter delight, she answered my email and agreed to send her clients my way for lodging, and I'd send her a kickback for each one. Same with the golf tournament next month. I also started some Facebook ads targeting Phoenix residents interested in Sedona, hoping to generate a few nightly stays.

An hour later, the phone dinged, announcing I had a reservation for the weekend, which I both appreciated and dreaded. Another chat with Ruby about her ability to move inanimate objects would be in order.

Now on to the lawyer. Google informed me there was a new attorney in town who also held an accounting degree and specialized in tax law.

Perfect. "Sounds like he'll know what he's talking about."

I filled out the online appointment request as my phone notified me I had another reservation. Suddenly, I felt much better about everything. Adam and I were moving in together. My best friend was getting married. I was slowly recovering from the business bomb Sylvia's death had delivered, and I'd finally addressed the tax issue. All of my completed tasks had kept me from wondering about the physical evidence that had nailed Pete.

"Look at you being all grown up," Ruby said from behind me. I jumped off my stool, not having realized she was there.

"You scared me," I muttered.

"Sorry about that. You found an accountant?"

She stared at me straight-faced, her voice so serious, I considered she was about to play some type of joke on me. Throw something at me? Show off a new ghostly skill she hadn't shared with me yet?

"Yes. He specializes in tax stuff."

"And from the sound of your phone, the reservations are coming in."

"Yes. You and I need to talk about our guests and your new ability."

Ruby grinned and crossed her arms over her chest. "I have a plan."

Uh oh. That never boded well for me. "I have a plan as well," I said. "And I promise you my plan is better." For me, anyway.

"I doubt it," Ruby said. "I'll go first."

"Fine. What's your idea?"

"You take me to Mr. Dimples' wedding, and I won't throw anything at any guests."

What a surprise. My grandmother wanted to behave? But her not tossing glasses at my guests wasn't enough. "You won't throw stuff? Can you do better than that?"

With a sigh, she rolled her eyes. "I won't move anything, either. I'll stay completely hidden while you have customers here. I'll even stay out of their rooms."

I narrowed my gaze, trying to ascertain if she was lying.

"I promise," she said, holding up her right hand as if she were about to swear on a Bible. "I really want to see Jack marry Darla. I'll be on my best behavior if you agree to take me."

Biting on my lower lip, I tried to think of a downside. No time alone with Adam on the trip was definitely one, but the plusses outweighed the negative. "Okay, let me think about it."

"Fair enough," she said, glancing around. "Things are changing. I can feel it in the air."

"What do you mean?" I hadn't shared that Adam would be moving in, and the fact that she hadn't mentioned it made me think she hadn't overheard our conversation.

"Darla marrying Jack is a big change. I feel like we've been moving down a one-way street and we haven't had any trouble with traffic. An inter-section is right around the corner and we're going to splinter off."

"What in the world are you talking about?" I asked.

She shrugged and shook her head. "Things can't stay the same forever. Time transforms us all."

As she faded away, I tried to understand her

riddle. Usually, she spoke so bluntly, there was no denying her meaning. A street? What street? And, she seemed so sad, which made my heart heavy, as well. With a sigh, I pulled out my paper bag containing the tea samples Wilder had given me and decided to go with the lavender. As I warmed the water in the microwave (my apologies to the British), my thoughts returned to Adam and the murder investigation. I was dying to know what the physical evidence was, and I hoped that he called so I could get some sleep. Otherwise, I'd be up guessing all night long.

With my tea ready, I went into the living room and turned on the television. After catching the end of the late-night news, I vowed never to watch it again. It left me with dread that the world would be ending at any moment. Absolutely depressing. At least my lavender tea helped to relax me a bit.

As I finished my cup, my phone rang. Adam.

"Hi," I answered. "Everything going okay?"

"Yes. Pete is adamant he didn't kill Sylvia, though. He's like a kid who got caught with his hand in the cookie jar and chocolate all over his face, but swears he didn't eat any cookies."

"What evidence did you find?" It must be pretty damning.

Adam lowered his voice. "The hammer. It had Tina's prints on it, just as you said it would, but Pete's were also all over that thing."

Huh. "So, Pete grabbed his hammer that morning and went and bashed in Sylvia's head? Then Tina picked it up when she found the body?"

"Precisely."

I recalled seeing Pete's hammer in his toolbox. "Why would he have two hammers? I saw one in his toolbox the other day."

"He's in construction," Adam replied. "I'm sure he's got dozens lying around."

Perhaps—yet nothing was fitting as neatly as I'd expected it to. "But where's Tina's hammer?"

"I think he killed her with Tina's hammer. Either that, or Tina misplaced her own and Pete used one of his. Who owned the hammer isn't important."

Not in my book. But he was the cop, not me.

Tina had been adamant the hammer found by Sylvia had been hers because of the condition of the grip. The hammer I'd seen in Pete's toolbox had also seen better days.

"And what about Wilder walking down the street that morning?" I asked. "It seems more likely he would've grabbed the hammer from Tina's yard and done in Sylvia."

"There's no physical evidence of it," Adam said. "Wilder had nothing to do with it." Except he had a devil-worshiping tattoo and an altar with Sylvia's picture. That certainly wasn't nothing.

"And what about Yolanda?" I questioned. "She probably had the easiest access to Sylvia because she lives next door."

"Doesn't make sense," Adam replied. "She goes across the street to grab the hammer, and confronts Sylvia in the garage?"

"Maybe. I'm just throwing out ideas." I sighed and considered another cup of tea but decided against it. I didn't want to make multiple trips to the bathroom throughout the night. "Do you think Tina did it? She could've killed Sylvia and started screaming, as if she was mortified by what she found."

"The timing doesn't work out. Sylvia was dead for a couple of hours before Tina found her. All the physical evidence points to Pete."

"Which is why Wilder is the perfect suspect," I said. "She was killed right around the time he was out walking."

Adam chuckled. "You're making me feel like

I'm not doing my job right."

"Sorry. I'm sure you've got the right person." But did I really believe it?

"Look, Bernie. Pete doesn't have an alibi. Says he was home alone. *His prints are on the murder weapon.*"

"But he lives alone. That's like me saying I don't have an alibi for the early morning hours, Adam."

"I'm usually your alibi," he said, snickering. "Or am I that forgettable?"

"Of course not!" I huffed. "I'm pointing out that just because someone lives alone doesn't mean that they killed someone!"

Voices in Adam's background drew closer— the sheriff and a female officer. "I need to go, Bernie," Adam said. "We're about to have another meeting on the case."

"Okay. Are you coming back here tonight?"

"No. After the meeting, I've got a couple more hours of paperwork, so I'll just crash at my place."

Disappointment settled in. Now that we'd decided to move in together, I wanted him home. At *our* home. "Okay. I understand."

"Goodnight. Love you."

"Love you, too."

I shook my head, confused. Tina had insisted

the murder weapon was hers. So, Pete had walked down the street that morning, picked up Tina's hammer, then marched into Sylvia's garage and killed her. And left the hammer there? Surely, he understood they'd look for fingerprints. Or perhaps he'd departed hastily and forgotten it?

"It's not my problem," I muttered as I stood and carried my empty cup into the kitchen. Elvira lay on the island, stretched out on her back, the tea bag of catnip torn to shreds. As she slowly turned her head toward me and stared at me through hooded lids, I realized she was completely high.

"Great. Now you're a junkie," I said, silently cursing myself for leaving the bag out. I should've hidden it again, but my mind had been elsewhere.

Despite my zoned-out cat, the catnip all over my counter, and my ghost speaking in riddles, things were going well. The murderer had been caught. Adam and I were taking a huge step in our relationship. Darla and Jack were leaping into wedded bliss. Customers would begin checking in the day after tomorrow and hopefully, I'd have an appointment with my new lawyer very soon.

So, why did I feel like I stood under a ten-story, teetering building about to crash on top of me?

CHAPTER 17

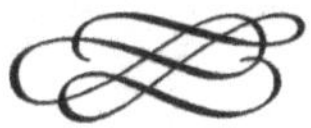

AFTER RETURNING from my morning run, Ruby met me at the door.

"You should only run if someone's chasing you," she said as I huffed and puffed hard enough to blow the house down.

"I think I did something to my knee," I moaned as I rubbed it.

"See? Now if someone does start chasing you, how are you going to get away with a bad knee?"

She had a point, but I chose to ignore her. Instead, I hobbled into the kitchen and motioned for her to follow me. After gulping down some ibuprofen with a glass of water, I sat down at the kitchen island. "I have something to tell you."

"What's up?" Ruby asked. She picked up my glass and set it down by the sink, then began giggling. "I'm so tickled I can move things around."

"Adam and I are moving in together."

Ruby arched an eyebrow. "Where? Here?"

"Yes."

She nodded and pursed her lips. "What's your mom going to say about that?"

My conservative parents would most likely have a hissy-fit, call me a sinner, and lecture me about giving myself away without the commitment of marriage. However, at thirty-five, I could make my own decisions. "They'll get over it."

"Probably not, but we can hope," Ruby grinned. "It'll be nice to see more hairy man parts around here."

She cackled as I rolled my eyes. More than once I'd caught her ogling Adam while he dressed. I'd never said anything because I didn't want him to know my lecherous grandmother watched him.

"This could be a lot of fun!" she continued. "Is he bringing Ned with him?"

Probably not. Especially since Ned had made it clear he wasn't fond of Ruby. "I don't know. We really didn't discuss him."

"I'm happy you're taking this next step," Ruby

said as she rounded the island and laid her hands on my shoulders. A chill traveled over me despite the sweat from my run. "The copper makes you happy, and that's all I ever want for you."

"Thanks, Ruby." I wished I could hug her and feel her thin frame wrapped in my arms.

"Now, let's break out the tequila so we can celebrate. Or, you can celebrate and I can pretend to."

"It's nine in the morning," I said. "I'm not drinking tequila. I'm having coffee."

"Party pooper."

As I brewed a pot, my phone dinged, alerting me to a text.

GOT *your message regarding your IRS bill. Please email me the letter along with the tax returns for the past two years. We can meet today at 4, if that works for you*

"THAT'S EFFICIENT," I murmured. Thankfully, I'd been very organized and was able to pull out my laptop, scan in the IRS letter, and find the tax returns in under fifteen minutes. I sent off the email and texted him back.

. . .

IT'S SENT and I'll see you at 4

I REALIZED I didn't know the name of the lawyer who I was meeting. Was there more than one in the office? Recalling my Google search, I didn't remember it being a multi-lawyer business. Glancing at the email address, it simply read: admin. "I guess I shouldn't care about a name as long as he or she gets my taxes lowered, right?"

"Exactly," Ruby said. "Not that I give a shake, but you never cleaned the Death Room. Luna's cooties are still all over."

"You're right. I'd better get up there and get it done." After grabbing my supplies, I headed upstairs. My knee still bothered me a bit, but not as much as before.

Luna hadn't had time to leave much of a mess, so the clean-up was easy and quick. Afterward, I took a shower, made myself a sandwich, studied other events coming to town, and contacted their organizers. By the time four o'clock rolled around, Ruby was climbing the walls with boredom and making my life difficult.

"How about a ride on the ATV?" she asked

hopefully. At first, I was going to say no, but then I realized I may be able to kill two birds if I drove the ATV to my meeting. It wasn't too far and I should be warm enough with a jacket.

"Sure. Please remember to mind your manners at the accountant's, though. Okay?"

"I promise," she replied, smiling sweetly. Which almost caused me to leave her at home. That grin usually meant nothing but trouble.

The ride to the office went smoothly, except for Ruby yelling at me to go faster, which I didn't do.

"No one's going to give you a ticket!" she yelled. "You're dating a cop!"

It wasn't a chance I was willing to take. In fact, since I was moving in with Adam, I felt I had to be extra cautious. I didn't want to be known as the law-breaker girlfriend. The sheriff had already accused me of murder more than once.

The office lay just off the main drag right behind Boots n' Bags, the custom leather store. I'd been eyeing a pair of boots in the window for a while now—high-heeled, black leather, thigh high with shiny baubles up the back. I fell in love with them until Ruby pointed out I would look like a stripper and I probably wouldn't be able to walk with the heel being so high. Besides, where would

I wear them? To the grocery store? It wasn't like I ever went anywhere requiring such fancy footwear. Then there was the fact I needed money for bills, not for fabulous boots.

The office was in a small building, one side being a dentist, the other now a lawyer. As I opened the door, the odor of disinfectant hit me and I wondered if the lawyer realized he'd be sitting in it all day long with the shared wall and probably ventilation system.

"Hello?" I called. Boxes lined the far-left wall. A credenza with a coffee machine sat to the right.

"He wasn't kidding when he said he was new in town," Ruby muttered. "He hasn't even unpacked."

Footsteps sounded from the back against the hardwood floors. "Sorry!" the approaching man said. "Welcome!"

As he smiled and outstretched his hand, I stood frozen, absolutely stunned. I knew this guy dressed in the navy-blue suit.

"Who is this?" Ruby said, moving in closer to him. "Do we know him?"

Tall with brown hair. Square jaw. Clean shaven. Yes, I had seen him before. But where?

"My name's Darren," he said, smiling. "I can smell your lavender perfume. It's nice."

I finally shook his hand. "N-nice to meet you," I said. "Do we know each other?"

He furrowed his brow. "I don't think so," he replied, gesturing around the office. "As you can see, I'm new in town."

"Huh. You look vaguely familiar to me."

"Well, hopefully that's a good thing. Why don't you come on back to my office? I've had a chance to look over the tax return and the letter you sent, and I have some ideas."

I trailed behind him. "Do you think you can help me?"

"Yes, I can. We're going to restructure your business and I'm confident I can get the tax bill lowered. There were some mistakes on your last return, which will help immensely."

His office was far more organized than the reception area. A computer sat on a large, wooden desk. The late afternoon sunlight filtered through the floor-to-ceiling windows over-looking a little patch of desert. File cabinets lined one wall. The whole room had been painted pale blue.

"This is nice," I murmured as I sat down in a chair in front of his desk.

"Thanks. Hopefully I can get the reception area put together in the next few days." After slipping on a pair of glasses, he glanced at his computer. "So, on this last return, you…"

His voice faded as I stared at him, the niggling feeling that I knew him still present. Where would I have seen him? The grocery store? Somewhere people wore suits. The bank? Maybe he'd been on a television commercial? Or I'd seen him online?

Ruby walked behind the desk humming some Janis Joplin. "Looks like he's married," she said. "Wife's a looker. Not as pretty as you, but definitely nothing to sneeze at." Horror came over me as she picked up a picture. "See? Isn't she cute?"

The frame hung just over Darren's head. *Please don't drop that.*

"Are you okay?" he asked. "You look a little pale."

"I-I'm fine," I said. "Please, continue."

Ruby snickered and set down the picture, then picked up another one. This time, she waved it over his head. "Woo… Woooooo… You look like you've seen a ghost, Bernie!"

With her antics, I'd never get through the meeting. I'd also realized long ago that the more I reacted, the worse her behavior became. She enjoyed watching me squirm with discomfort and worry.

"I'm going to bang him over the head with his hot wife!" she cackled, now holding two picture frames.

Shooting to my feet, I bit my tongue to keep from yelling at my ghost. "I... I need to use the restroom," I said.

Darren startled and slowly removed his glasses. "Uh... sure. Out the door, to the right."

I extended my pointer finger as I stared at Ruby, hoping to convey she better put down the pictures because I was leaving the room and she had no choice but to follow me.

She set them down without finesse, causing Darren to turn around. "That's weird." He picked up the one face down. "I wonder how that happened?"

Hurrying from the room with my ghost in tow, I found the restroom and entered, quietly shutting the door.

"You need to stop this!" I hissed. "You promised me you'd be good!"

"No, I didn't!"

I took a deep breath and shut my eyes for a moment. When I didn't want to strangle her, I opened them. "Yes, you did promise me you'd act like the dead adult you are. Now, this is important. I need you to stop with the antics so I can concentrate on what he's saying, because if I don't get this taken care of, I'm going to lose the house. Do you understand?"

Why did I always feel I was the grownup with my grandmother's ghost?

"You're right. I'm sorry. I got carried away."

"Thank you. Now, I'm going back in there and you're going to remain silent."

"I will."

"And you won't move anything, nor will you pick up anything."

"Fine. Okay."

After exiting the bathroom, I smiled as I entered Darren's office again. "Sorry about the interruption. I really had to go."

Ruby snorted as I sat down.

"That's okay," Darren said, setting his glasses back on his nose. "As I was saying…"

"Oh, wow," Ruby said, this time from behind me. It wasn't like I could look over my shoulder. I'd already caused enough distractions… Well, Ruby had. If she wasn't dead, I'd want to kill her.

"Houston, I think we have a problem," Ruby continued. "A big one."

"So, if we restructure the business in this format, it's going to lower your future taxes significantly," Darren said.

"That's wonderful," I replied, relief sweeping through me. "And you have a plan for the current tax bill?"

"Yes. I just need to you sign some papers giving me permission to talk to the IRS on your behalf. He tapped on his computer keyboard, then stood. "Let me grab them from the printer. I'll be right back."

I glanced over my shoulder as he left, then stood and hurried over to Ruby, wishing I could throttle her. "Did I not just ask you to please be quiet?"

"Look." She turned a picture frame my way. I stared at the image for a moment, then stepped back.

"That's... that's Darren."

"And..."

And someone who looked identical to him, except very different. No wonder I'd thought I'd recognized him.

The picture had been shot from the waist up. Darren stood next to his mirror image, their arms around each other's shoulders. While one man wore a white golf shirt, the other donned jeans and a dirty red t-shirt. Brown hair on both, except one had a scar under his left eye and a scraggly goatee. Darren, the polished one, Cody the bedraggled.

"That's Cody," Ruby said. "Sylvia's ex-husband."

"You're right," I muttered, goosebumps traveling down my spine and over my arms. I recalled the night Luna and I found him in Sylvia's house, heartbroken. The tears, the proclamations of love. *'To be close to all that's left of her,' he'd whispered. 'To smell her favorite perfume. To touch her pillow again. To... to try to be as near to her as I can for just a little while longer.'*

"Quite a coincidence, isn't it?" Ruby asked just as Darren strode into the room.

"Ah. I see you've found the picture of me and my twin," he said, taking a seat behind his desk.

I nodded. "And he was married... to Sylvia?"

Darren's brow furrowed. "Yes, he was. Did you know them?"

"No." I sat down, suddenly feeling terribly uncomfortable, but I couldn't pinpoint why. "Well, sort of. I'll sign those papers so I can get out of your hair."

He slid them across the desk along with a pen.

After scribbling my name, I stood. "Thanks for all your help."

"Of course. It was nice to meet you, Bernie."

As he walked me to the front door, I asked, "I'm sorry about Sylvia's death. I'm sure Cody was very distraught."

Darren laughed as he pushed open the glass pane. "Not at all. That woman was the bane of his existence. It's unfortunate she was murdered, but his life became a lot easier when Sylvia died."

CHAPTER 18

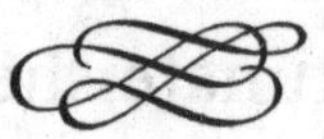

"Why do I feel so weird about that meeting?" I asked as Ruby and I straddled the ATV and I stared at the accountant's office. My old friend, anxiety, clenched my stomach while it felt as if bugs crawled over my skin. Discomfort didn't begin to describe the uneasiness flowing through me in tormenting waves. The urge to leave the area was strong, yet, I couldn't seem to put the ATV into gear.

"Because it's weird when you think there's only one copy of a person, but there's actually two. And you've met one of the copies before, but you didn't even realize it. Serious mind games, I tell you. Reminds me of when I used to have one too many shots of tequila. Psychological warfare."

With a heavy sigh, I started the ATV and headed out of the parking lot. A heavy chill ran down my spine as Ruby leaned her ghostly form into me.

"Sounds like Cody was pretty happy Sylvia bit it," Ruby continued. "I still think he did it. It's always the crazy ex."

"No, it wasn't. Adam verified he had an alibi. Remember? He spoke to the barista and the coffee shop owner in Cottonwood and identified Cody was there that morning. It wasn't him."

"What if it was Darren at the coffee shop?" Ruby said. "Just thinking out loud here. But Cody doesn't seem like a foo-foo coffee drinker. He's more of a black coffee, Folgers guy. But Darren, he's a different story. He's a latte with flavoring type of man. What if Darren was at the coffee shop, Cody knew that, then killed Sylvia and used Darren as an alibi because they look so much alike?"

Sylvia had left Cody—motivation for a crime of passion. He'd been married to her long enough to be familiar with her schedule and would be aware of her early morning hours. All he had to do was lie in wait until she exited the house to the garage, then... bam! "But that doesn't explain the prints on the hammer," I said. "They found Tina's and Pete's. No one else."

Ruby shrugged and sighed. "You're right. Physical evidence would trump my theory. But it's always fun to play the devil's advocate. Just a thought I had."

And a good one. What if they had the wrong man in custody? Was I going to let my neighbor take the fall for a crime he didn't commit? Spend years in prison? *But what about the physical evidence that nailed Pete, dead to rights?*

"What if Darren killed her?" I mused.

"But why?" Ruby asked. "He doesn't have a motive. And don't forget those pesky fingerprints you keep mentioning."

Dang it. She was right, but something niggled at me. At the next light, I flipped a hard U-turn.

"What are we doing?" Ruby asked.

"We're heading back to Darren's office. I have questions."

"You're going to confront the lawyer about his brother?"

"Exactly."

"Are you sure this is a good idea, Bernie? I mean, this could be very dangerous."

"When have you ever cared about danger?" I asked.

"You're right!" My ghostly grandmother whooped and shouted. "Danger's my middle name! Bring it on!"

Moments later, we pulled into the parking lot once again. A woman was leaving the dentist office and a white pickup truck sat illegally parked in front of Darren's.

"Must be his next appointment," Ruby said.

"We shouldn't go in until that person leaves." After shutting off the ignition, I crossed my arms over my chest, ready to wait, despite feeling like a target sitting out in the open. I should've driven the SUV.

"Nonsense." Ruby said. "I have a plan."

I groaned and shook my head.

"Relax. You won't even step foot in Darren's office. They'll never realize you're there."

I turned to my grandmother. "And where will I be?"

"At the dentist. I'll go through the wall and see what I can find out, then report back, if I see or hear anything out of the ordinary."

"And if you do?"

"We'll call Adam."

I didn't see any way for her plan to go sideways this time. "Okay. Let's go."

We hurried across the parking lot to the dentist office. I stepped inside as Ruby ghosted through the shared wall to the lawyer. I smiled at the receptionist, staying as close to the adjoining wall as possible.

"Good morning," she greeted me, her smile warm and bright—and so very white. Their products worked well. "Do you have an appointment?"

"He's here with his brother!" Ruby shouted, her voice only slightly muffled. The walls must have been paper-thin. "That truck belongs to Cody, not a customer!"

"Um... no," I said. "I was hoping to get some pricing for a cleaning." I inched over to the wall and placed my head against it. If I could hear Ruby, maybe I'd catch some of the brothers' conversation.

As the receptionist rattled off some numbers, the brothers' voices did filter through the wall. "Sylvia's house is mine," Cody said. "She blackmailed me into co-signing on it. I have every legal right to it."

"Well, maybe you shouldn't deal drugs and she wouldn't have had anything to blackmail you with," Darren said.

"It was either co-sign or she'd turn me in," Cody replied. "I wasn't about to go to jail."

"Are you okay?" the receptionist asked.

I brought my finger up to my mouth and scowled at her as I attempted to catch more of the conversation.

"We may have a new neighbor," Ruby shouted. "Sounds like Sylvia's house belongs to Cody now."

"I'm sorry, but I'm going to have to ask you to leave," the receptionist said. "I'm not sure what you're doing, but you need to go." As she stood and pointed at the door behind me, my irritation grew. I needed to hear what was being said!

"They're going in back!" Ruby yelled. "I can't follow!" She appeared in front of me. "Come on! You can sneak in there and hear everything yourself instead of listening to this one. *'Please leave. You need to go.'* You should punch her in the face before we head next door."

Fear caught in my throat. Although it seemed to be comprised of papier-mâché, the wall did offer some type of protection against the brothers. Sneaking into the office left me open to all sorts of bad things that may happen... if I was caught.

"Come on!" Ruby yelled. What had happened to me staying out of sight? To calling Adam at the first sign of trouble?

"Please don't make me call the police," the employee insisted, picking up her phone.

"Gosh, she's annoying," Ruby muttered, but if in her shoes, I'd call the cops as well. My behavior was anything but normal.

Before I could think through Ruby's plan and come up with at least a hundred reasons as to why I should head home instead, I said, "Sorry to have bothered you. That won't be necessary. Have a lovely afternoon." Then, I hurried out the door and snuck into Darren's office. As I tried to calm my breathing, I searched for a place to hide. Ruby ran ahead—well, fifteen feet ahead—then turned and shot me a glare.

"Come on," she whispered. "Let's go."

As I followed her toward Darren's office, sweat broke out on my brow and my hands shook. What in the world would I say if I was caught?

"So, if I sell the house, I'd be completely out of debt," Cody said. I stopped and leaned against the wall where I had their doorway in my sights, but they wouldn't be able to discover me—unless they came out.

"And you won't start gambling again, right?" Darren asked sternly. "Don't forget, you owe me money as well."

"I know, man. I know. Things are finally turning around for me, though. But I do miss Sylvia. It hurts."

"She was toxic, Cody," Darren said, annoyance dripping from his voice. "Remember all the stuff she put you through. Remember the black eye she gave you, the time she locked you out of the house when it was snowing, and her slashing your tires just a couple of months ago."

"We had some good times," Cody said wistfully. "It's those I miss. Did you know I broke into the house?"

"You broke into her house?" Darren asked, his voice incredulous. "Don't tell me. I don't want to know."

Well, technically, if Cody was truly one of the owners, it wasn't illegal entry, but I wouldn't correct anyone and give away my position.

"Yeah, it's probably best that you don't," Cody said, chuckling. "But know this, my brother: my life is turning around. I loved Sylvia and when she cheated on me, it destroyed me. All I could think about was getting revenge, and that put me in a bad place."

"He played us all," Ruby shouted, throwing her hands in the air.

But had he? Everything I heard cast him in a

guilty light. However, the physical evidence deemed him innocent. One couldn't fake finger-prints... could they?

"You also cheated on her first," Darren said. "Don't forget that. You aren't the victim here. You need to stop with that. Take responsibility for your actions, Cody."

"All right."

"Sylvia was a horrible, abusive person during your marriage and cheated on you after you did her wrong. Then, she divorced you because you had a baby with another woman, and you developed a gambling problem. All of that is on you. You should've left years ago."

"Shut up! I get it!"

"Just making sure. Your whole life you've blamed others for your problems. You're forty. It's about time you—"

"Shut up, Darren! You're worse than Dad! I'm out of here. I can't take your lecturing."

"Wait a minute, Cody. You know I'd do any-thing to help you, right? I only want to see you happy. That's it."

"I know."

"You're my brother and I want you to have a good life."

"And that's starting right now," Cody said. "No matter how much it hurts, Sylvia's death has been a blessing in disguise. It's the best thing for me."

"I'm glad to hear you say that. I love you, little brother."

"You're older by two minutes, Darren. Quit being so darn sentimental." They both chuckled and I imagined them in a brotherly embrace. "I've got to go."

Crud. I hurried toward the front door, sure I was going to be caught.

When I pushed it open and was about to breathe the fresh scent of freedom, Darren called out, "Bernie?"

"Busted," Ruby said. "But you'll be fine. You've had self-defense classes. You can bounce these two off the walls."

My ghost had far more confidence in my abilities than I did. I most certainly could not bounce anyone off any wall... maybe a good kick to the groin and elbow to the face, but no one would be bobbing off any walls.

"What are you doing here?" Darren asked.

As I tried to think of an excuse, I carefully studied Cody. Confusion crossed his face, then his gaze widened. He recognized me.

While his features settled, I said, "I thought I left my sunglasses here."

"They're on top of your head," Darren replied, chuckling.

"Really?" Ruby muttered. "Your sunglasses?"

It was the best I could do. I smiled and pulled them off. After tucking them into my coat pocket, I made some sound that I hoped resembled a laugh. To me, it sounded like a choking whale. "Silly me. Thanks, Darren."

Cody narrowed his gaze and if Darren hadn't been present, he'd have frightened me. Cold and calculated, and at that moment, I had no doubts he was capable of murder.

Before anyone said anything else, I hurried outside and hopped on the ATV. As we drove home, my hands shook while the adrenaline slowly ebbed.

Had Cody killed Sylvia? The circumstantial evidence pointed to it and he certainly had the most to gain. Was Pete truly innocent? And if Cody had killed her, what about the fingerprints on the hammer? Adam had said they belonged to Tina and Pete. Tina had touched the hammer, so I understood why hers would be there. But Pete? The only reason had to be because he'd handled it. And if he'd held it, didn't that mean he'd murdered her?

My gut and the circumstantial evidence pointed to Cody. All of it. But that dang physical evidence was messing with my theory. What was I missing?

CHAPTER 19

As I PACED my living room, I had the feeling something was right in front of me that would unravel the mystery of who had killed Sylvia, but I simply couldn't see it.

"It's so frustrating!" I yelled. Elvira, who rested on the back of the couch, opened one eye and then turned away from me. She detested loud noises, but apparently not enough to give up her perch.

"Stop yelling!" Ruby screamed. "What are you trying to do? Wake the dead?"

"Aren't you funny," I muttered, then issued a long litany of curses as I picked up my phone to call Adam.

"Hey, Bernie," Adam answered. "What's up, hot stuff?"

"I don't think Pete killed Sylvia," I replied, not in the mood for flirty banter.

He sighed, a sound I recognized of him about to become highly annoyed with me. "Why is that?"

"Because of her ex-husband."

"Cody?"

"Yes. He's not as nice as you think he is." I mentioned the gambling problem, the money he owed, that he was a drug dealer, and the fact he was now the owner of the house. "His life changes with Sylvia dead, Adam."

"Circumstantial. We have hard evidence that Pete murdered her. Prints on the hammer, remember? We've got a motive—they were sleeping together and she was hassling him about the tree. And we've got an alibi for Cody."

"Well, they actually had an affair," I said. "You make it sound like everything was on the up and up when they were involved. Pete wasn't aware she was married."

"Fine. They had a sordid affair. That's the least of his sins. Pete's not a boy scout, Bernie. He's done time before."

No, I hadn't been aware of that detail. "For what?"

"Bar fight. Put a guy in a hospital a few years back."

The revelation shouldn't have surprised me, but it did. People never fit in the little boxes I thought they should, and I was finally beginning to learn that.

"He's got a history of violence, so that's a bonus in our case," Adam continued. "We've also got motive and opportunity. It's a slam dunk for us."

When he put it like that, Pete was guilty without a doubt. "Yes, yes. I understand all that. Did you know Cody has a twin brother?" I asked.

"I didn't, but I'm not sure what that has to do with anything."

"What if that wasn't Cody at the coffee shop? What if it was his brother?"

The long stretch of silence had me wondering if we'd been disconnected or he'd simply hung up. "Adam?"

"I'm here. That's... it's an interesting thought, but it doesn't negate the physical evidence, Bernie."

I sighed and attempted to quell the frustration swelling within me. The last thing I needed was to become short-tempered with Adam. "Are you coming over tonight?"

"Please don't be snappy with me," he said softly. "I can hear the irritation in your voice."

I'd failed miserably. "I'm sorry. There's just something that's not adding up for me."

"The case has been solved, Bernie. Everything has added up just as it should."

"Okay. Fine." I'd have to put Sylvia's murder behind me. "What about tonight?"

"I'd planned on being over right after work," he said. "Want me to pick up some food?"

"Yes." I certainly didn't have the desire to mess around in the kitchen and try to make something edible. And dishes... yuck.

"What are you in the mood for?"

"Probably sandwiches from the deli or Chinese."

"Your wish is my command. I'll see you later."

After hanging up, I decided to go for a walk—not a run. My knee still bothered me a little and I didn't want to do any further damage.

"Do you want to go with me?" I asked my ghost.

"No, thanks," she said. She and Elvira had curled up on the couch together, my cat purring loudly. "This is much more fun than exercise."

She wasn't wrong, and for a second, I debated stretching out on the other sofa and indulging in an afternoon nap. "Okay, I'll be back in a bit." Best to evacuate the premises before I could change my mind.

As I strolled down the street, I glanced at all my neighbors' houses. Yolanda was most likely out back in her pseudo-forest enjoying being naked in nature. I hadn't seen Tina recently. Maybe she tended to her gardens in back. And then there was Wilder... I still hadn't seen Luna and his house appeared to be empty. Perhaps he was searching for his next sacrifice to Satan. I stopped in front of Pete's and crossed my arms over my chest. How much time would he spend in prison? Did he have a good lawyer? What would now happen to his house? With no family I was aware of, would it be foreclosed? Had he *really* been a killer? As much as the evidence pointed to the answer being a resounding yes, I still had a hard time swallowing it.

With a sigh, I continued my walk, then headed back home after two miles out. A four-mile walk had to be somewhat equal to a two-mile run, and I didn't have the pressure on my knee. Bonus, for I still didn't feel any better.

My gaze was once again drawn to Pete's

house. I stopped and stared. What was it about this place that had me so fixated?

"Bernie!" I glanced over my shoulder to find a smiling Tina approaching wearing gardening gloves and a toolbelt that carried small shears, her phone, and a couple of shovels. Very handy. "What're you doing?"

What was I doing? Studying a potential killer's house trying to figure out why I was obsessed with it. "I'm... I'm not sure."

She shook her head and crossed her arms over her chest, mirroring my stance. "It's hard to imagine one of our own as a murderer. I've done my own fair share of contemplation about it."

"He had motive," I said. "His fingerprints were found on the hammer."

"Very true."

But so were Tina's.

What if Pete wasn't the killer, but Tina? Adam had said they'd investigated her, but nothing came out of it. Yes, Sylvia had hassled her about her gardens, but she couldn't claim an affair like Pete could. To my knowledge, she also hadn't told Sylvia to drop dead.

I had to investigate Pete's house further. Something wasn't sitting right with me, and my gut told me his home held the answers I was looking for. I could only hope I'd recognize them if I saw them.

The secret to solving the murder niggled annoyingly right at my conscious.

"I'm heading home," I said, forgetting my walk. "I'll speak to you later."

"Sure, hon. Take care."

Maybe I was wrong to not willingly accept the official physical findings, but I wouldn't stop poking around until I was satisfied.

WHEN NIGHTFALL CAME and I waited for Adam, I stared out my front window monitoring my neighbors' whereabouts. Yolanda had gotten home not too long ago and her living room lights blazed brightly. I imagined her settled in for the night with a cup of tea and a book.

Although I couldn't really get a good view of Tina's, I knew she was an early riser and would most likely be in bed very soon.

Every light seemed to be illuminated in Wilder's home, and I didn't know what to make of it. No one had seen Luna yet. Maybe he needed the light to finish her grave in the backyard.

Regardless, my street was empty, and it was

time for me to make a move. "Are you coming with me?" I asked Ruby.

"Heck, yes! I wouldn't miss this for all the tequila in Mexico."

"That's a lot of tequila," I replied, snickering. "You sure about that?"

"Don't make me second-guess myself. Let's go! Cagney and Lacey are on the move!"

As we hurried toward Pete's house, she said, "You know, we need one more hot chick and we could be Charlie's Angels!"

Rolling my eyes, I didn't bother to comment. The less noise I made, the greater the chance I wouldn't be discovered.

I glanced around, then jogged up Pete's driveway, still unsure of what I searched for. After making my way around the side of the house, I peeked in the windows as Ruby ghosted through the walls. Nothing struck me as odd, and my grandmother wasn't any help.

"This guy needs to clean his toilet," she said. "Absolutely gross."

As I stood on the porch, I glanced around and debated venturing into the backyard. Beer cans were strewn about. A plate with an old sandwich sat on the table. How the bugs hadn't gotten to it yet, I didn't understand. I almost tripped over his toolbox.

With a gasp, I knelt next to it, a hedge of bushes hiding me from the street. The hammer protruded from the side, along with a wrench and a handsaw. Organization wasn't Pete's strong point. I studied the hammer grip, ripped up from use, just as Tina's had been. This was it, what I had been looking for! I wasn't sure how it all fit together, but I knew the hammer was crucial to finding the real killer.

As I was about to grab it, vehicle lights swung around, illuminating the area.

"Abort! Abort!" Ruby yelled. "Someone's here!"

"Are you sure?" I hissed. "They aren't just parking on the street?"

"Nope. They're walking up the driveway! Hide!"

"Who is it?"

"I don't know! I left my night vision glasses at home!"

"Ruby!"

"Crawl over there! To your left! Behind the bush!" Small scrubs had been planted along the side of the front porch, but had yet to mature.

I did as instructed and quickly realized the single bush did nothing to hide me. If I curled up in a ball, I could be seen over the top. If I laid flat, it hid my head and my upper torso. My only hope was that whoever approached didn't glance my way and notice my legs.

Footsteps sounded up the driveway, and I was out of time. There wasn't anywhere to hide.

"Holy cow!" Ruby yelled.

I peeked around the leaves to find a man hunched over the toolbox, a phone in his hand lighting the area. He grabbed the hammer and stood.

"What the heck is your lawyer doing here?" Ruby asked.

Great question, but everything suddenly fell into place. I'd found the killer.

I scrambled to my feet. Darren's eyes widened as he attempted to hide the tool behind his leg.

"B-Bernie! What are you doing here?!"

"I live in this neighborhood," I said, stepping around the bush. "But I guess you didn't pay much attention to that when you looked over my tax return. Details are important, Darren. I think the question is, what are you doing here, in my neighbor's yard, stealing his hammer?"

He chuckled and shook his head. Even in the low illumination of the flashlight, the resemblance between him and Cody was uncanny.

Darren was simply a bit more polished. "I don't know what you're talking about."

I pointed at him and narrowed my gaze. "You killed her, didn't you?"

For a brief second, acknowledgement flashed in his eyes, but his condescending smile returned once again. "Are you drunk?"

"Oh, how I wish!" Ruby said. "I'd give just about anything for a few shots of tequila and a beer chaser!"

"You killed Sylvia," I said, ignoring his question. "And I'm going to nail you for it."

How, I wasn't sure. But, I'd eventually get it all figured out. My mind raced in the attempt to do so.

"Listen, Bernie," he said, taking a step toward me. "I'm not sure if you're on drugs or drunk or you're just crazy. But I didn't kill anyone."

"Uh oh," Ruby said. "We have a problem. He's gripping that hammer pretty hard, Bernie. Don't push him, or you may end up with it stuck in your skull!"

I pulled one of the chairs in front of me as Ruby bent over. Darren would have to climb over it to get to me. Running wasn't an option. In front of me lay the chest-high wedges. If I turned, I'd trip over the small shrubs hiding in the darkness behind me.

He stared at me, probably going over the pros and cons of bashing in my head, just as he'd done to Sylvia.

Ruby rose to her full height with a large wrench in her hand. Thankfully, she stood behind Darren so he wouldn't notice. With a guttural yell, she lifted it up over her head and slammed it into Darren's.

As he fell to the cement like a sack of potatoes, I yelled, "Why in the world did you do that?"

"Preemptive strike," she said, dropping the wrench. "He was either going to run or try to do you in. Neither plan worked for me." She reached down and pulled out a roll of duct tape from the tool chest. "Now, let's hog tie this pig and call Adam."

CHAPTER 20

AFTER RUBY and I hauled Darren into a chair, I taped his arms to the armrests and ankles to the legs, then called Adam and put him on speakerphone.

"I've got the killer," I said. "I'm at Pete's house. I need you to come right away."

"Excuse me?"

"There's no time to explain!" Ruby and I shouted in unison. We traded glances then I concentrated on the phone. "Pete's innocent. I have the murderer. Get over here, now! Please!"

"Hang up and don't give him a chance to answer!" Ruby said.

I did and took a deep breath. If I was wrong, the lawyer would be coming after me. Legally, certainly, and physically, probably. According to Ruby, he'd about beat me over the head with a hammer. How in the world would I explain that? I rubbed my face and groaned. My ghost had most likely saved me from an assault, but she'd sent me from the frying pan into the fire.

While we waited, Ruby hummed and stared at Darren. "Why are the lawyers in your life either conniving villains or dead?"

"I have no idea," I sighed. But Darren's shenanigans reminded me that now that he'd been rendered unconscious and I'd accused him of murder, he most likely wouldn't be helping me with my tax issues.

Ruby nodded. "Maybe when you go and see the next lawyer, you should ask if he's planning on killing anyone."

As Darren groaned, I debated hitting him over the head again until Adam arrived.

"What's happening?" he slurred.

Ruby picked up the wrench, but thankfully, Darren hadn't opened his eyes and seen the floating tool... yet.

I heard a car pull up and motioned for Ruby to set it down before glancing around the bushes. Relief swept through me when I discovered a police cruiser. Adam hurried up the driveway, his phone flashlight illuminated.

"What the heck is going on here?" he asked, his gaze bouncing from me to Darren while he placed his hands on my shoulders. "Are you hurt?"

"Thanks to Ruby, no."

"Ruby? What did she do?"

"She thought he was going to slam me over the head with a hammer. She got to him first with a wrench."

Adam let out a slow whistle. "Okay. Start at the beginning and tell me everything. I've got to figure out a way to explain Ruby's antics so the situation makes sense."

After taking a deep breath, I began. "Pete being the murderer was just too neat and tidy for me and I really started to question the theory. Why would Pete walk toward Sylvia's, pick up Tina's hammer, and then attack her in her garage? Without wearing gloves or even trying to wipe down the hammer? Also, he works construction. I bet if we went through his house, we'd find half a dozen hammers. Why steal Tina's?"

"To have more than one set of prints on it?"

I shrugged. "Maybe."

"But go on."

"The one person who wins the most in Sylvia's death is her ex-husband, Cody. Hands down. I overheard him and his brother Darren speaking. Cody gets the house. Sylvia blackmailed him to co-sign on it."

"Then why don't you think Cody did it?"

"Honestly, he's just not smart enough," I said. "And, I do think he truly loved Sylvia, despite getting another woman pregnant."

"She's right," Darren said. I hadn't realized he'd woken. "Cody did love that woman with his whole heart, so when she divorced him, his life went on a downward spiral. Booze, dealing drugs, gambling... the divorce ruined him."

"Sir, are you admitting you killed Sylvia?" Adam asked.

Darren sighed and shut his eyes. "I shouldn't talk to you, but I'm so tired of trying to cover this up. Yes, I did. I killed her and framed Pete for the murder."

"Why don't you tell me everything?" Adam said, pulling the other chair up so he faced Darren. "From the beginning."

I crossed my arms over my chest as I listened and admired our taping job. He wasn't going anywhere.

After Cody had his affair and Sylvia discovered it, she changed. "She became spiteful, hateful, and just all-around nasty, especially to Cody," Darren said. "I tried to keep my nose out of it, but the constant toxicity slowly ate away at Cody, and that hurt me. I hated seeing my twin like that."

When Sylvia announced she would be leaving Cody, that had done him in. "The drinking, the drug dealing, the gambling... he was on a path of complete self-destruction. I did my best to help, but he needed closure. Then, Sylvia blackmailed him to co-sign on the house and moved on the same street as the man she'd slept with. I couldn't believe it. At first I was horrified she'd do such a thing to Cody."

"She wasn't aware Pete lived here," I said. "It was a coincidence. According to Pete, they had no idea where the other lived."

Darren shrugged. "It doesn't matter. I saw my opportunity to help Cody."

I recalled what he'd said in his office: *You know I'd do anything to help you, right? I only want to see you happy.* Apparently, that included murder.

"An opportunity to avenge your brother," Adam said.

"Avenge? No. I'm not some superhero. I just

wanted to give him peace. A chance to start over in a good place financially without Sylvia on this earth."

"How did you know Cody would have an alibi?" I asked.

"He goes to the same coffee shop every single morning. They know him there by name. I was aware he'd be suspect number one, so I needed him to be safe. Sylvia always had the early morning shift. She and Cody would leave the house around the same time. I killed Sylvia when I knew Cody would have a rock-solid alibi."

"He sure benefits from her death," I said. "That's super convenient."

Darren smiled. "He deserves it. She blackmailed him to get him to co-sign for the house. If he didn't, she'd go to the sheriff about his drug dealing. He could either sign or go to jail."

Adam sighed and pulled out his notebook from his back pocket. "From the beginning on the day Sylvia was killed, Darren. Run it through for me."

Darren hadn't parked on our street, but around the corner. After jogging over to Pete's, his initial plan had been to steal something from Pete's car to kill Sylvia. But then he noticed the toolbox sitting on the porch with the hammer sticking out. With gloves on, he grabbed it and hurried down the street to the scene of the crime.

Then, he waited until the garage door opened, walked in, and killed her. For a moment he considered moving her, which was why her limbs were stretched out into a star-shape. Instead, he decided to leave her there. He set the hammer down and left.

So, let me get this straight," Adam said, rubbing his face. "You took the hammer from Pete's toolbox, killed Sylvia, left it at the murder scene for the police to find... and then what?"

"I realized Pete may notice his hammer was missing. If he did and then discovered Sylvia had been killed with a hammer, I was worried he'd leave the area. A little digging revealed he'd had a violent past and had done time before. I wanted him to suffer for what he did to my brother. After I killed Sylvia, I grabbed the hammer lying in the neighbors' yard over there and replaced Pete's with it."

"Pete went down for the physical evidence," Adam muttered. "It was almost a perfect setup, except Bernie wasn't buying any of it."

I nodded, pride swelling within me. I'd just saved a man from prison.

"All I wanted was to help my brother," Darren

said. "No one would miss Sylvia. She'd turned into such a horrible person, people would be glad she was gone."

"No lies there," Ruby said. "All her neighbors certainly were."

It was true. She'd threatened all of us in some form or another, and no one on my street would miss her in the slightest bit.

Which I suddenly found quite sad. Unexpectedly, I held compassion for the dead woman, and I hoped she rested in peace.

"I have one question," Derek said. "Who hit me from behind?"

"It was me, turd face!" Ruby yelled as she danced a little jig. "You got bested by a dead lady!"

"You were hit from behind?" I asked. "I don't think so. I was the one who smacked you with the wrench."

Darren's brow furrowed in confusion as if he was trying to remember the altercation.

"Sir, you're under arrest for murder," Adam said, standing. He stared at Darren for a moment. "As soon as I figure out how to get you free of all this duct tape."

EPILOGUE

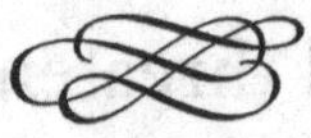

WEEKS HAD PASSED and my neighborhood had gone back to the quiet, tranquil place it had been before Sylvia moved in.

Cody had put her house up for sale, and I could only hope someone nice bought it. I'd seen a couple of families looking at the property, and I always waved and smiled, hoping to convey friendly people lived on the street and we'd like more of the same to occupy the house.

It turned out that Wilder wasn't a serial killing Satan worshipper, but a witch in love with Luna. I'd seen them out and about many times together.

"You owe him an apology," Ruby said as we watched the two walk past our house, hand-in-hand, heading out into the desert.

"I know, I know. But he threatened to get a re-straining order on me if I came near him again."

"I'm sure he'll change his mind when he real-izes you want to apologize." The two lovebirds stared into each other's eyes, smiling as if it was the best day of their lives. "Go now. They're right in front of the house."

With a long sigh, I opened the door. Hope-fully, I wouldn't ruin their perfect day. "Wilder!" I called as I trotted down the walkway after them and waved.

They stopped as I approached. "I told you I didn't want you near me," Wilder said.

"And I came to apologize. I'm sorry for ac-cusing you of killing women."

"What?" Luna said, her mouth slightly opened.

"You were asleep when this went down," Wilder said. "I never told you about it because the negativity was so awful. I didn't want you to suffer with me."

"Oh, Wilder," she whimpered. "You poor thing! Thank you for protecting me, but you shouldn't have to go through that alone!"

"It's okay, honey," he said.

Jeez. You would think I'd come at him with a gun, sword… or a hammer.

"Look, I just wanted to apologize." Suddenly,

an idea popped into my mind. "And I was wondering if you could help me."

"With what?" he said, his voice wary. "You also asked for my help when you accused me of being a serial killer."

"My friend's getting married. I wanted to do something nice for her... a special gift. I was wondering if I could buy a gift basket for her? Maybe some nice soaps, bath salts... things like that? You make those as well, right?"

He nodded and asked when the wedding would be held.

"A couple of months."

"Okay, I'll see what I can do. I'll be in touch."

I smiled and turned back to my house. I'd made peace with my neighbor. Adam would begin moving his things in this weekend. And my best friend was getting married. Life was perfect. What in the world could go wrong?

ALSO BY CARLY WINTER

Sedona Spirt Mysteries

Bernie and the ghost of her dead grandmother find themselves in the middle of various murder investigations. Danger and hilarity ensues as the crazy duo follow the clues to discover the killers.

The Tri-Town Murders

Complete Series

Follow newspaper reporter Tilly and her group of fun, quirky friends as they solve murders in a fictional, small town in California.

News and Nectarines

News and Nachos

News and Nutmeg

News and Noodles

Killer Skies Mysteries

Set in 1965, join Patty Briggs, stewardess extraordinaire, as she flies the skies and solves murders with the help of her friends… and one cute FBI agent!

ABOUT THE AUTHOR

Carly Winter is the pen name for a USA Today best-selling and award-winning romance author.

When not writing, she enjoys spending time with her family, reading and enjoying the fantastic Arizona weather (except summer - she doesn't like summer). She does like dogs, wine and chocolate and wishes Christmas happened twice a year.

For more information on her books, please visit: CarlyWinterCozyMysteries.com